Accidents can happen . . .

Coralynn's face tightened into an expression of rage. Gobs of mustard were all over her, dotting her white sweater with huge yellow blobs.

"I think you've helped me enough for one day," she snapped at Paula, and stalked off toward the ladies' room.

"Hey, don't worry, Paula — it was an accident," Garth said.

Paula smiled apologetically. She was searching for something to say when suddenly all conversation in the room stopped.

The sound of wailing rose through the silence.

The wails turned into screams.

That awful noise was coming from the ladies' room, Paula realized.

Were those screams of fury, she wondered . . . or pain?

**Other Point paperbacks
you will enjoy:**

THE WAITRESS

Sinclair Smith

SCHOLASTIC INC.
New York Toronto London Auckland Sydney

ISBN 0-590-45063-8

Copyright © 1992 by Dona Smith
All rights reserved. Published by Scholastic Inc.

12 11 10 9 8 7 6 5 4 3 2   2 3 4 5 6 7/9

Printed in the U.S.A.   01

First Scholastic printing, March 1992

For Larry and the Old Town crew, and with thanks to Greg and Jean

7

Chapter 1

I'm going to scream, thought Paula.

She watched as the thin, birdlike figure of a man paced frantically back and forth in front of her, making wild, frenzied gestures.

He's insane, she thought helplessly. If I have to listen to his raving for one more minute, I'll lose my mind.

The real torture was his *voice* . . . that horrible screeching. Fingernails scraping against a blackboard was the only way to describe the way it made you feel.

I'm trapped . . . for now, she realized. Besides . . . what happens when he finishes his little speech is even worse. She could feel her terror mounting as the clock ticked relentlessly on.

Best not let him know what I'm thinking . . . best not make him angry.

She gazed around the room at the faces with their glazed, vacant expressions. *He* did this to us, she thought. We're all his victims. Never mind . . . it will all be over soon.

* * *

"Oh!" Paula gave a little shriek and jumped back in her seat, startled out of her reverie.

The frantic little man was bearing down on her with his beady, bespectacled gaze.

"Do you think you'd find our little sessions more entertaining if you paid attention, Miss McLaughlin?" he asked smugly. "Would you repeat the current assignment for us?"

"S-sorry, Mr. Woods," Paula stammered. Color flamed into her face as she heard the class snickering around her. "I guess I just drifted off for a minute."

"Well, then, please rejoin us in our discussion of the current assignment on suspense," he snapped as he returned to the front of the room.

Paula sighed with relief. Yes, she thought, until the end of this class period we're all victims of this madman — Mr. Aloysius T. Woods, English 373.

Is it possible to die of boredom? she wondered, glancing at the clock. I know he's killing me.

"For example, consider Alfred Hitchcock's *The Birds*, based on the story by Daphne du Maurier," Mr. Woods said as he resumed his usual pacing. "We all see birds all the time, and we hardly take any notice, do we? But if the birds suddenly attack you — well, that's something else again, isn't it? Something quite unexpected." He paused, looking at the class triumphantly, as if he'd just said something very clever.

"So, as you review your assignment I want you to keep *The Birds* in mind and think about other things — even people — and what your reaction would be if they did something unexpected — something out of the ordinary. The baby-sitter, the cleaning lady, the janitor — these are people we all take for granted, don't we? But if the baby-sitter tries to burn down the house and the cleaning woman tries to smother the children in their beds, that's something else again. Just imagine finding out that the janitor is an international terrorist — wouldn't that be *unexpected*?" His voice screeched to a maddening crescendo.

I've been daydreaming too much in here lately — I really ought to pay attention, Paula thought uneasily.

Somehow, though, it had been getting harder and harder to concentrate on anything. . . .

I hate this school, she said to herself angrily. And I hate this town, and I hated moving here and starting over in October of my junior year.

Don't worry, you'll make new friends, Mom had said. Paula laughed to herself. I wouldn't have a friend in the world if Coralynn Hailey had anything to say about it, she thought, glancing behind her at the tall, slim girl with pale blonde hair who sat in the next row.

She could feel Coralynn's icy blue gaze slashing into her back.

Coralynn hated her.

Why?

Because of Garth, Paula answered herself, remembering the day she had been struggling with her locker and he came over to help. He had joked about her frustration — laughed and patted her arm as if to comfort her. Had he let his hand linger on her shoulder for a moment? Paula thought so, but she wasn't sure because then . . .

"Garth!" The name had rung out like a shot from across the hall. Paula had turned and recognized Coralynn, leaning insolently against the wall.

She had been watching them.

So what if Garth is Coralynn's boyfriend? Paula thought, feeling defensive. We weren't doing anything — he was just trying to be friendly.

Of course, I wouldn't mind being more than friends with Garth Zvecker. A lot more than friends, she admitted to herself.

Coralynn usually gets her way, Garth had told her. Paula shuddered. More and more lately, it seemed as if Coralynn were spying on her — following her around. She seems to just appear from nowhere sometimes, Paula thought incredulously. I look behind me — she's there. I turn 'round a corner — she's there — wearing that smirk on her face. Just when I don't expect it — she sneaks up on me . . . usually when I'm alone.

Paula laughed to herself. Well, maybe I should do something unexpected, she thought.

Something to make Coralynn sit up and take notice.

Something to make Coralynn know what it feels like to be threatened.

The idea made her feel positively gleeful.

She sighed. It sure would be nice to get rid of Coralynn — for good.

She glanced at the clock again. Time was running

out, and she had more important things to think about.

She had one class left after this one. At 3:15 it would be over, and then Paula would have to begin her first day as a waitress at Trixie's Dog House — FOR DOGGONE GOOD CHOW, as the sign promised.

She felt her panic increasing. I'll be in the doghouse, all right, when Trixie finds out I don't know the slightest thing about waitressing. But if I hadn't lied a little, Trixie probably wouldn't have hired me.

The bell rang, releasing the prisoners.

Why, oh, why did I ever take this job? Paula agonized as she gathered up her books. No doubt about it, she thought nervously, it was going to be a real nightmare.

Chapter 2

Paula hurried as she caught sight of the Dog House sign. A neon puppy stood over the doorway, wagging its tail. It barked the words *BOW WOW WOW* endlessly. That dog would probably tear you to shreds, she thought grimly.

"Hiya, hon, glad you got here early," Trixie, the owner of the Dog House, greeted Paula as she rushed through the door and deposited her books on the counter.

Paula grinned as she looked at Trixie. Why on earth does she want to dress that way? she wondered.

The fifty-something woman sported the same outfit worn by the waitresses at the Dog House — bobby socks and saddle shoes, pink flared skirt, white frilly blouse with black piping, and black apron. There was a lacy handkerchief in her pocket, and fastened above it was the Dog House puppy on a name tag. "Hi, my name is TRIXIE," it said.

Well, I suppose in here, Trixie looks almost normal, Paula thought, glancing around the restaurant.

It's like being in a time warp, back in the 1950s she thought. A long Formica counter stretched along one wall, lined with yellow vinyl-covered stools. The floor was covered with black and white linoleum squares. There were several rows of booths, and even a jukebox in one corner. It's almost like being in a movie, she concluded.

Hanging behind the counter was a black felt board with white letters that advertised the daily specials. "TRIXIE'S SURPRISE," Paula read.

Trixie patted her red beehive hairdo. "Guess you're wondering about the uniform." Her red lips stretched into a smile. "That's in case I have to stop flippin' burgers and run out of the kitchen to pitch in and help the waitresses. Besides," she grinned, "it's kinda fun, makes me feel young again. You know, I started working here after I quit high school. I attended beauty school for a while," she said patting her hair again, "but it wasn't for me, so I dropped out and started waiting on tables. Now I own the place." Trixie winked. "Come on, we'll go over the menu," she said, sliding into a booth.

"Great," Paula replied, sliding in across from her. She tried to look happy and confident. Be pert, perky, and personable, she told herself.

But Trixie suddenly looked stern. "You said you knew about waitressing, so you should catch on real quick," she said.

What happened, she was so friendly a second ago, why is she scowling like that? Paula wondered uneasily.

"That's good," Trixie continued, "because when

customers start pouring in this place is a madhouse, just a madhouse. Anyone who doesn't know what they're doing would just be — killed." She smiled.

Paula nodded weakly. This is going to be worse than I thought, she wailed inwardly.

"Now here's our menu . . . you take one, too." Trixie smiled and held out the menu to Paula as if she were awarding her a prize.

"Now listen," she said, scowling again, "all the burger platters are called BOW WOW, see?" She pointed to the list. "A plain burger is naturally a plain BOW WOW, for cheeseburger you write C-BOW WOW . . . makes it faster, get it? For a double burger with everything you write BOW WOW *WOW*, and the frankfurters — we call them wiener dogs, so you just write WIENER."

Wouldn't it be faster to write DOG? Paula wanted to ask — but something about Trixie's face warned her not to. "I think I've got it so far," she said softly. How can anyone say this with a straight face, she wondered, glancing at Trixie's tight-lipped expression. When the customers order they must sound like a chorus of spaniels.

"Well, go ahead, *say* it, hon," Trixie urged, her eyes shining brightly. "You've got to call out the orders, not just write 'em."

Paula took a deep breath.

"B-BOW WOW," she stammered. "BOW WOW *WOW*."

By the time Trixie finished outlining the duties, Paula's head was reeling with details. Yes, she thought, it's much, much worse than I ever imagined.

"I guess that's it," Trixie said brightly. "Since you've done this before, I'm sure I don't need to explain any more — do I?" She looked pointedly at Paula, her penciled eyebrows raised.

"I guess I'll be okay." Paula smiled weakly. She knows I've never been a waitress, and she's toying with me, she decided.

"Great," Trixie said, smiling broadly. "Because now I want to talk about *accidents*. I tell all my girls to be very, very careful about accidents. You have to be on the lookout every minute for things like stuff falling in the ice, and grease on the floor."

Trixie jumped out of the booth. "You can't imagine how many accidents are just waiting to happen in a restaurant, if someone is careless — or stupid. We don't want anyone choking" — she grabbed her neck — "or slipping" — she kicked a leg in the air — "and falling and cracking their head open, getting blood all over the place" — she hit the side of her red beehive with her hand. "Okay, that's it." She grinned.

Thank goodness — I don't want to see any more, Paula thought. This is definitely weird. I wonder if they taught her to style that beehive in beauty school. . . .

"Follow me downstairs, and I'll show you where to change," Trixie said sternly.

I really don't want to go down there, Paula thought, but she obediently followed Trixie down the narrow stairs. There's something scary about this lady — but what is it? One minute she looks as if she's my best friend, and the next she looks as if she's going to slap me.

The cellar was lit with one unshaded bulb. At the far end, behind a partition, Trixie showed Paula the area for changing clothes. Quickly, Paula threw on the uniform and shoes as Trixie chattered away.

"That looks real good," she said as Paula appeared from behind the partition.

Looking around, Paula noticed two huge boxes with thick walls and heavy doors at the other end of the cellar. They look almost like some sort of torture rooms, she observed. "What are those, Trixie?" she asked, pointing.

Trixie seemed suspicious. "You've been a waitress before and you've never seen those things?" She raised her penciled eyebrows. "I'm surprised — every restaurant has at least one. Well, come on, I'll show you. You might as well know where everything is." Trixie walked over to one of the big boxes, opened the door, and stepped inside. "It's a refrigerator. Well, don't just stand there, come on in."

Swallowing hard, determined not to show how scared she was, Paula stepped in. She found herself surrounded by shelves full of fruits, vegetables, and other supplies. In the middle of one wall, near the ceiling, a fan whirred.

"Don't ever let yourself get locked in here," Trixie chattered brightly. "You'd suffocate pretty fast."

"Doesn't that fan vent to the outside?" Paula asked, puzzled.

"Well, you don't see a window, do you, hon?" Trixie chuckled. "That fan just blows the cold air around. Okay, follow me and I'll show you the freezer."

They left the walk-in refrigerator, and soon Trixie was motioning Paula into the other box. "See," Trixie explained as she stepped behind Paula. "It looks exactly like the refrigerator inside — except it's much colder."

Then the door slammed shut. Trixie had locked Paula inside the walk-in freezer — alone.

This is *insane*, Paula thought, through her fear. This woman locks me in a freezer because I don't know how to *wait on tables*?

Chapter 3

Paula stood shivering inside the freezer. Through the door she could hear Trixie giggling on the other side.

"Hey, what's the idea?" Paula said, banging on the door with her fist.

"I just love to play this joke on first-timers," Trixie was chuckling outside. "Everybody's so scared of these things the first time they see them — you can always tell. Scared to death of getting locked inside.

"But there's no need to worry, hon," Paula could hear Trixie saying brightly as she listened desperately through the door. "Just look down there along the door on the left — there's your safety handle."

Yes, yes, there it is, Paula thought with relief. She pulled the handle and walked out. I'm free, thank goodness, she thought, sighing to herself.

Trixie was smiling broadly and chuckling. She seems to be having a great time, Paula thought resentfully.

"Now you'll never be afraid to come in and get

something you need," Trixie chortled.

Sure, not if you tie me up and hit me over the head first. Maybe I really am going crazy. Why is this woman acting as if locking me in a freezer is a joke? Paula wondered as she followed Trixie up the narrow stairs.

Then she caught sight of her reflection in the mirror at the top of the stairs. She smiled. Not bad, if I do say so myself, she thought, noticing the way the pink and white set off her long chestnut hair and hazel eyes and the way that the skirt hugged her narrow waist. Maybe I'm going to like this job after all.

Trixie turned to Paula. "You've never been a waitress . . . why'd you lie about the job?"

"I thought you wouldn't hire me if you knew I didn't have any experience," Paula confessed. "Besides . . . I catch on fast," she added hurriedly.

"Why, sure you will, hon," Trixie said with her red-lipped smile. "Everybody's got to start somewhere. I think you're real spunky. Okay, you're on your own. Go ahead and set everything up. Virgilia should be around here someplace. She'll give you a hand. The kid has a brain as big as all outdoors."

"Thanks, Trixie," Paula replied, stepping behind the counter. What a whale of a sense of humor this lady has, she thought as she ripped open a bag of coffee. What's the next lesson, locking me in the dishwasher?

"Well, there's that Cookie, here at the last minute as usual," Trixie remarked, shaking her flaming red head.

Glancing out the window, Paula saw a girl drive up on a motorcycle, with a boy hanging on behind her. She parked the bike and removed her helmet, shaking loose a raven-colored cap of curls.

"Cookie . . . I've seen her around school."

"Cookie around *school*," Trixie said, rolling her eyes in mock surprise. She laughed. "I thought Cookie had better things to do than go to *school*. Listen, hon, keep that last booth over there open for my niece, okay? It's your table and she always likes to come in and sit there with her friends," Trixie said as she walked back to the kitchen.

"Oh . . . yeah." Paula nodded absently, her eyes on the girl outside. Cookie was leaning against the boy, saying something animatedly.

Cookie's one of the wildest kids in school, Paula thought, smiling to herself. She admired the carefree way Cookie acted, laughing and flirting with all the guys — even Garth. I wish I had the nerve to wear those clothes, she thought enviously.

Suddenly Paula was jolted from her daydream by the realization that coffee was spilling from the machine all over the floor. What do I *do*? she thought frantically.

"Hey, take it easy," a voice chirped behind her as someone placed a pot under the scalding stream of liquid.

Paula turned and saw a short, freckle-faced girl with a pleasant owllike expression.

"I'm Virgilia Radner, they call me Virgil," the girl said, extending her hand. "Anything you need help with, just ask. The first few days here can be pretty scary. You're Paula, right?"

"Yes, and thanks. You're not kidding about things being scary. Trixie already tried to lock me in the walk-in box."

"Oh, come on," Virgilia laughed. "You know she was only kidding. She always does that. You don't really think she was going to leave you there, do you?"

"Well . . . no." I guess I really went off the deep end, Paula thought.

"Anyhow, here's the first hint," Virgilia said. "When you flip the *start* switch on one of these things, make sure there's a pot under it."

"Right," Paula replied, feeling foolish.

"How're you guys doing?"

Paula turned to see Cookie walking in, motorcycle helmet in hand.

"Hi, I'm Paula. I'm fine . . . so far."

"Really? They'll fix that," the girl joked, indicating with a wave of her hand the parking lot where cars were starting to drive up. "I've got to go and change. See you later — and don't worry, this job is a piece of cake."

I'm not convinced, Paula thought as she ran around filling containers of salt, pepper, mustard, and ketchup. What else? She paused, suddenly feeling uneasy. Somehow she sensed that someone was there, watching her. She turned around quickly.

"Coralynn!"

The blonde girl looked surprised at first — but

then a smirk spread over her face. "Well, well, well," she drawled. "I didn't know you got a job at my aunt's resturant, Paula."

Oh, no, Paula wailed inwardly as the realization hit her. *She's* the niece.

"Hi, Aunt Trixie." Coralynn waved sweetly. "Can we have our regular booth?"

"Sure, hon," Trixie yelled from the kitchen. Paula hurried over to set their table. I hope she chokes, she thought.

Coralynn was wearing dangling earrings that looked like big pieces of sushi, Paula noticed as she watched the girl stroll toward the booth.

"Hi, Paula, how's it going?" said a voice behind her.

Paula turned. "Garth . . . hi!" He's so gorgeous, she thought as she gazed at the lean, muscular build . . . the way his blond hair fell over his forehead as he leaned down to speak to her. I'm staring, she realized, feeling foolish.

"Good luck with the job," Garth called as he slid into the booth beside Coralynn.

Coralynn regarded Paula coolly. What does he see in that — witch? Paula wondered as she bustled away.

The restaurant was getting really busy now — people were pouring in. Paula busied herself waiting on customers, putting off the trip to Coralynn's table, when she felt a light tap on her shoulder.

"Better get with it," Cookie said. "Ice Princess is waiting to order you around — I mean, waiting to order," she winked.

Here goes, Paula thought, approaching the table. She could hear Coralynn whining at Garth from several tables away.

"I mean, now you're taking a class in *painting*? Give me a break."

They didn't notice her for a moment, but then Coralynn turned to Paula with a sneer. "We've been waiting. Thanks for paying us a visit."

As Paula took their order, she wondered if Garth held her gaze just a little longer than he had to — or was it just her imagination.

Please, please, please, don't let anything go wrong, she begged silently.

When the food for Coralynn's table arrived, Paula delivered it and left as quickly as possible. I hope that's the last I hear from them, she prayed. But suddenly a loud commotion came from their direction.

"Wow! Somebody knows I *love* salt," Garth was chuckling as Paula hurried over. She saw that his plate was covered with a mound of salt.

"Top fell right off," he laughed, indicating the empty salt shaker and top on the table.

"Hey, don't worry, Paula — it's no big deal," he said good-naturedly, shaking salt off his burger. "Really, it's no big deal," he said again, looking fixedly at Coralynn.

"Well, *I* think it's a big deal," hissed Coralynn. Her face had tightened into an expression of rage. Gobs of mustard were all over her, dotting her white sweater with huge yellow blobs.

"Let me guess . . . you didn't screw the top on

this either, right?" She glared at Paula as she held out the mustard container.

"Oh, no . . . I'll get towels!" Paula said frantically. She ran for the ladies' room. Naturally, this is the perfect time for the dispenser to be empty, she thought as she rummaged around. Serves Coralynn right, though, she couldn't help thinking with satisfaction. She found some paper towels in a cabinet under the sink and hurried back to the table where Coralynn sat, still seething.

"Sorry," she said lamely, handing her the towels.

"I think you've helped me enough for one day, thank you," Coralynn snapped as she stalked off toward the ladies' room.

"Hey, don't worry, it was an accident," Garth said in sympathy after she left.

Paula smiled apologetically. She was searching for something to say — when suddenly all conversation in the room stopped.

The sound of wailing rose through the silence.

The wails turned into screams.

It took Paula a moment to figure out where the awful noise was coming from. The ladies' room! she realized, as she stood there frozen in shock.

Were those screams of fury, she wondered . . . or pain?

Chapter 4

There were murmurs of "What the . . ?" and "What in the world . . ?" as people jumped from tables and booths and surged toward the screams. A crowd was forming around the tiny hallway that led to the ladies' room.

Suddenly Coralynn's best friend, Lizzie, burst through the crowd with another girl in tow. They raced into the ladies' room, slamming the door behind them. After a few moments the screams subsided and the three girls emerged from the restroom, whispering among themselves.

The crowd milled around waiting to hear what had happened. Lizzie had her arm around Coralynn, who was sobbing softly and shaking her head. "The handles . . . switched . . . suddenly scalding me," Paula heard Coralynn choke out through her sobs.

Then Coralynn quieted down. She drew her breath in sharply and glared at Paula. "Somebody switched the hot and cold water handles. I could have gotten badly *burned*," she spat furiously. "You were in there long enough . . . YOU DID IT!" she said, pointing an accusing finger.

I wish the floor would swallow me up, thought Paula helplessly. It was horrible. Everyone was staring at her.

The worst thing was the expression on Garth's face.

Skeptical.

Suspicious?

Coralynn was playing the scene to the hilt. Trixie rushed out of the kitchen to check her over.

"Hon, you're shaken up, but you're not hurt at all as far as I can see," she said finally.

As the crowd dispersed, Paula saw Trixie standing at the kitchen doorway, staring at her. Paula waited. After what seemed like forever, Trixie turned and went back behind the grill.

How could this have happened? Paula wondered unhappily. Then it dawned on her. Coralynn wasn't really hurt . . . she planned the whole thing to get back at me, she thought furiously.

Would Coralynn really do that?

Yes, she told herself firmly, she would.

"How was your first day at work?" Cookie said with a wink as they cleaned up later.

"My worst nightmare!" Paula replied, sighing wearily. "That business with Coralynn — I know she planned the whole thing somehow, and managed to make it look like I did it."

Cookie looked at her in surprise. She hesitated

thoughtfully for a moment before saying anything.

"Paula, you're overreacting, or exaggerating, or something," she said, shaking her black curls. "I mean, the girl was upset about her sweater — and maybe she's a little stuck-up — but I'm sure the whole thing will be forgotten by tomorrow. The idea that she *planned* to make it look like you did it is just plain — crazy."

"*Really*, Cookie," Paula replied. "You should see the way she follows me around school — spying on me."

She stopped suddenly when she saw Cookie staring at her with a bewildered expression on her face. She had to admit that it did sound a little strange.

"It could be that I'm just stressed out," Paula said finally, shrugging her shoulders.

"Well, don't be too hard on yourself." Cookie grinned. "To tell you the truth, this job is no picnic for anybody the first few times. You'll get the hang of it — you've just got to relax."

"Thanks," Paula said gratefully. "But," she added slowly, "it's not just the job. It's not easy starting in a new school after the year's already begun — and moving, leaving my friends. See, my dad died last year, and for months my mom hardly did anything. Then all of a sudden she threw herself into this flurry of activity. She got this high-powered job here, and we had to move. As a matter of fact, she was just called out of town on business — she may be away for a couple of weeks."

"Hey — that sounds pretty good to me!" Cookie chuckled. "Seriously, though," she said sympathetically, "it sounds like you've gone through a rough time.

"But listen," she said, tossing the sponge and catching it as she spoke, "the kids here aren't so bad once you get to know them — even Coralynn. I'll personally see to it you get introduced. I know! Coralynn's having a party soon; that would be a great place to meet everybody."

Paula gasped, before she realized that Cookie was kidding. They both dissolved into laughter.

"Really," Cookie said, trying to calm down. "You wait and see. I think I can fix things up between you and Coralynn. I can handle her," Cookie said confidently. "Besides, who cares what Coralynn thinks? She gives great parties."

" 'Bye, ladies!" called Virgilia, heading for the door. "And Paula, forget about Coralynn. She's a . . . a brat," she said as she exited. " 'Night."

Maybe I've been blowing this thing with Coralynn out of proportion all along — turning her into a monster, Paula thought later as she tossed and turned in bed. After all, Cookie and Virgilia didn't seem to think the whole thing was such a big deal. She punched her pillow lightly and turned over again.

As Paula drifted into a restless sleep, she remembered what Cookie had said about fixing things up with Coralynn, knowing how to handle her.

What did Cookie mean? Paula wondered, falling into slumber.

Chapter 5

As the next few days went by Paula tried not to think about Coralynn — or Garth, but sometimes she couldn't help it. Especially in Mr. Woods's class.

Stop it! Paula shouted silently to herself. Stop daydreaming and pay attention! Think English class! But no matter how she tried to keep her attention focused on Mr. Woods, her mind kept drifting back to the incident at the Dog House.

At least I'm getting the hang of the job, she thought. I guess I have Cookie to thank for that. She's really been a big help.

Paula smiled to herself, thinking of how friendly Cookie had been.

In the past week, Cookie has introduced me to more people than I've met since I've been here.

Working at the Dog House is a good way to meet people, too. But there always seems to be something a little weird going on there — like that message a customer found scrawled on a napkin the other day — *Think you're funny? YOU JUST MIGHT DIE LAUGHING!* And then there was that red dye in the hand-washing soap in the ladies' room. The poor girl looked like her hands were covered with blood.

Paula stared out the window and continued to ponder the strange goings on at the Dog House, her eyes fixed on some invisible point beyond the horizon. The teacher's voice became a distant hypnotic singsong.

Snap! Mr. Woods's ruler cracked on the desk inches from Paula's hand, causing her to sit bolt upright in her seat.

"Oh, Miss McLaughlin." Mr. Woods's voice sliced into her consciousness. "I see we are fighting a losing battle with our daydreaming once again." He smiled with exaggerated sweetness.

Titters from the class.

"Everyone, bring in your responses to the question at the end of the chapter on Monday. *Dismissed!*" Mr. Woods whisked his briefcase under his arm and swept out the door.

Oh, no — *what* chapter? she thought helplessly.

The bell rang and students started departing quickly. Somehow, each time Paula tried to catch someone's attention, she just missed them. There's Julie what's-her-name, I'll ask her, she thought, hurrying after a lanky girl in a blue sweater.

But Coralynn blocked her path. What now? I've had enough from her, she thought, pushing past.

"Wait! Listen, we've got to talk." Coralynn came running after her, her face bright and eager — a little tense. "I want to apologize for the way I acted," she said. "I guess I got carried away — it wasn't right. Will you forgive me?

"Anyway," the girl rushed on, speaking quickly, "I know it's kind of short notice, but I want to invite you to my party on Saturday night. Come on, don't you have the Dancercise class for gym next period?"

"Well, yes," Paula replied hesitantly. What's she up to? she wondered. This is too good to be true.

"Come on, I'll tell you about it while we walk to class. It's nothing fancy," Coralynn continued. "My aunt's letting me have it at the Dog House, and the whole gang's going to come. You come, too — and we'll really and truly be friends." She smiled.

"Are you kidding?" Paula asked, incredulously. I don't know if I even *want* to be her friend at this point, she thought. Still —

"I'm serious," Coralynn said solemnly. "Cross my heart," she said, making an elaborate gesture.

"Done, then — thanks," Paula said, shaking hands. "Coralynn, by the way," she said as they headed for the locker room, "did you catch the English assignment . . . the chapter he was talking about?"

Coralynn smiled. "Sure," she said. "You pick one of the essay questions at the end of chapter five."

"Thanks," Paula said, walking to her locker. It looks like things are going to be okay, she thought happily.

Later, though, as Paula warmed up to the music in class, the doubts returned — but she forced herself to dismiss them. She didn't want anything to spoil her good mood. Forget what happened before — everything is going to be fine now, she told herself cheerfully, stretching toward the ceiling.

The music was speeding up now, and Paula got caught up in the rhythm. The class always made her forget whatever she was worrying about.

Dancing isn't Coralynn's thing, she noticed, watching the blonde girl's clumsy movements. She sure puts a lot of energy into it, though. Paula stifled a giggle. The movements are supposed to be graceful, she thought . . . but Coralynn looks like a drowning person signaling frantically for help.

Cookie! she thought, suddenly. Of course — Cookie must have talked to Coralynn and straightened everything out.

Where *was* Cookie, anyway? Paula scanned the room. She must've cut class *again* . . . but why?

That was the last thought Paula remembered before she felt a stabbing pain in the side of her head. Then everything went blank.

Chapter 6

"Hi, Paula!" Coralynn gave an excited little yelp as she opened the door of the Dog House. "Hey, everybody, the party can really start. The guest of honor has arrived!" She yanked Paula by the arm, pulling her along.

Paula felt suddenly lightheaded. A pale, silvery light bathed the party guests in an eerie glow. The room seemed to spin like a merry-go-round. Everything was blurry and confused. She pressed her hands to her temples.

"My head . . . it hurts."

"Oh, dear," Coralynn said cheerily. "It must still hurt from when you fell in gym class.

"Oh, well," she gave a little wave of her hand, "a party is just what you need to take your mind off that nasty old headache. We've been waiting for you to be the first to try the punch." She propelled Paula to the center of the room where the guests were all standing around a crystal bowl.

Something is wrong, Paula thought as she felt Coralynn's grip tighten. There was something about the way Coralynn and her friends were all wearing the same weird, crazy grins . . . and their eyes glittered.

"No! I don't want to go first. Let me out of here!" Paula yelled as she started to struggle.

The guests began to chant, "TRY THE PUNCH! TRY THE PUNCH! TRY THE PUNCH!"

Her face was being forced down, down into the red liquid until it was covering her face. She fought for air as her breath bubbled to the top in a little stream.

Then a horrible realization struck her. It wasn't punch at all, it was blood!

As desperately as she struggled, she could feel herself slipping . . . getting weaker. If I don't get air, I can't hold on much longer, she knew.

Just when Paula thought it was over, the pressure on the back of her neck suddenly stopped, and she was able to raise her head. She collapsed onto the floor and propped her head on her arms, inhaling huge gulps of air.

"Punch! Punch! No, no — punch!" Paula mumbled deliriously as she looked up into the faces surrounding her.

They seemed to be trying to talk to her, but she felt as if she were rolling along in a sea of noise.

"Get back, ladies, and give her some air. She's coming to! That was quite a whack on the head you got, miss," Paula heard someone saying far away. She opened her eyes and blinked. Why are the lights so bright? she wondered.

Then she saw Ms. Christiansen's face. I'm in the

gym, she realized. She could feel the hard floor beneath her back.

Something happened — and I fell.

"Ow — my head hurts," she groaned, pressing a hand to her forehead.

Coralynn was bending over her, scowling. "Well, of course I didn't punch you, that's ridiculous! How dare you say that!" She stamped her foot.

"You heard her, Ms. Christiansen. She accused me of punching her. It was the first thing out of her mouth!"

Ms. Christiansen was regarding Coralynn with a cool stare.

"Hey, Coralynn, you sure whacked her!" A voice piped up from the back of the crowd.

"WHO SAID THAT?" Coralynn demanded, craning her neck this way and that, searching for the offender.

What is everybody talking about? Paula wondered.

Coralynn looked flustered for a moment. Then she rearranged her features into an expression of concern.

"I was so worried about you. It was an accident, you know. Everyone was jumping — and then we had to turn. I was in front of you and somehow we bumped into each other. Then you fell down."

Ms. Christiansen stared at Coralynn again. She looked as if she was thinking about something.

"Listen up, everybody," she said finally. "Let this be a lesson. *Watch* what you are doing at all times. Be aware of the person in front of you, behind you, and on either side of you. An accident can cause serious injury just the same as if it were done on purpose." She looked pointedly at Coralynn.

"Now go ahead to the showers!" The teacher clapped her hands, and the girls began filing toward the locker room.

Paula cradled her head in her hands.

"Want me to call your folks?" Ms. Christiansen asked.

"No, no," Paula murmured. "My mom is out of town on business, anyway." She stood up slowly. It took some effort to keep her balance.

Coralynn rushed to Paula's side. "I'll help you! Look, Ms. Christiansen, I'll take care of my friend," she said eagerly.

"Well, I don't know." The gym teacher looked skeptical.

"Pleeeeeease," Coralynn whined.

"Maybe if you'd just help me into the locker room, Coralynn — I'd like to get changed," Paula said weakly. This whole thing is an accident, it has to be, she told herself. The room was crowded, everybody was getting into the music — maybe not paying too much attention to what they were doing. It might have been as much my fault as Coralynn's.

"Okay," Ms. Christiansen agreed. "Coralynn, go ahead and help Paula — but for heaven's sake, be careful."

Coralynn took Paula's arm and began to lead her toward the locker room.

"I want you to stop into my office before you leave, Paula. You're going to see a doctor, just in case . . ." the teacher called after them.

"All right!" Paula called back. Ow — it hurts to raise my voice, she realized suddenly.

Coralynn helped Paula get her things out of her locker. Paula dressed, moving in slow motion. She still felt a little dizzy. After she finished dressing she combed her hair gently, careful to avoid the bump on her head.

Coralynn appeared silently behind her. Paula saw her reflection in the mirror. She had a bright smile on her face.

"I hope the doctor says you're all right," she said. "I wouldn't want *anything* to keep you from coming to my party."

Chapter 7

Saturday morning Paula sat up in bed and stretched cautiously.

No sign of a headache yet, she thought. Yesterday it had been terrible, as if someone were banging pots and pans together inside her head.

The doctor told her it wasn't serious but said she should take it easy.

What time is it, anyway? she wondered, turning to look at the clock.

Just then the phone rang. She stretched out her arm and answered it without getting out of bed.

"Hello?" She knew her voice still sounded thick with sleep.

"Hey, sleepyhead, rise and shine! It sounds like you're still in the sack. It's Cookie."

"I guessed," Paula said, pulling the covers around her.

"Anyhow," Cookie continued, "I thought I'd take you on a tour of the town — if you're okay, that is. I heard you took quite a dive in gym the other day."

"Yeah, I stayed in bed all day yesterday — it

was pretty bad. I hated to take off from school."

Cookie chuckled. "Really? I bet you didn't miss much. So . . . what do you want to do?"

"Well," Paula hesitated, "I don't know about going out. I've got chores to do, and homework to catch up on."

"Come on, it's Saturday. I can have you home in plenty of time for homework and chores."

"Well, let me think." Paula fidgeted. She glanced at the clock. Nearly eleven already! If she went out there was no way she'd have time for everything she had to do, and Coralynn's party was tonight. Somehow she didn't think Cookie worried very much about homework and chores. But she *had* been in the house all day yesterday, and she was a little stir-crazy. I'll catch up on things tomorrow, she decided suddenly.

"Okay, I'll meet you. But, Cookie — not the motorcycle, okay? I'm too shaky to handle it."

"No problem," Cookie laughed. "I planned on bringing the car anyway. I'll pick you up in half an hour, exactly."

Cookie was true to her word and arrived in exactly half an hour, which was a bit of a surprise to Paula. She hadn't expected Cookie to be strict about time.

For the next hour they drove around town with Cookie pointing out various spots of interest: the mall, the bowling alley, where to buy concert tickets, etc.

"There's Scoop's," she said, pointing to a small brick building with a red roof. Above the doorway a smiling clown held an ice-cream cone in each hand. "Sinfully good ice cream, and a great place to go when you don't want to be seen in the Dog House, if you know what I mean." She winked.

"Well, I guess I don't know what you mean," Paula confessed.

Cookie shook her head. "Paula, Paula — it's where you go with date number two when you don't want to be seen by date number one. Except that it's pretty hard to keep a secret in this town, since Scoop's and the Dog House are basically the only two high-school hangouts there are," she laughed.

"Great," Paula said grimly. She looked at Cookie out of the corner of her eye. She seemed so sure of herself — she was pretty, funny, and popular. She treated life almost like a big game. But there was something else about Cookie, too, a kind of tension Paula could see sometimes, under that carefree manner. It was as if Cookie were trying a little too hard to have a good time.

"Cookie, what's the story with that place?" Paula asked as they passed a drive-in restaurant. "It looks like it's closed — but how could a place close down in this town, with only two places to go?"

Cookie seemed not to hear the question. "Hey, did you decide to go to Coralynn's party?" she asked after a moment.

The story of the drive-in probably isn't very interesting, anyway, Paula said to herself, and let the subject switch to Coralynn's party. "Well, she invited me after all, and she says she wants to be friends, just like you said. What in the world did you do to convince her?"

"I scared her to death," Cookie laughed. "Seriously, I didn't do anything. I told you, Coralynn may be spoiled, but she's no monster. And she not only gives great parties, she gives *loads* of parties."

"So you don't think she's up to something — some kind of trick?"

"Honestly, Paula, absolutely not. Besides, Garth will be there, somehow I think you might be interested to know," she said with a meaningful glance.

Great, everybody's probably noticed I'm interested in Garth.

Now it was Paula's turn to change the subject. "I'll tell you what I'd be interested to know — it's what happened to you in Dancercise that day I had the accident. I know I saw you in school earlier, and you have that class with me, but you weren't there."

Bad choice of topics, she realized instantly as a look of annoyance came over Cookie's face.

"Who are you, a detective or something?" she snapped.

"I'm sorry — I didn't think it was a big deal," Paula said softly, taken aback.

"Look, I'm sorry, I don't know what's the matter with me. I guess I know I shouldn't cut classes, but I've got a lot on my mind. There are just some things I've got to think through. I don't want to go into it now, but I'm sorry, really."

Cookie had turned slightly to face Paula and had

momentarily taken her eyes off the road — something that was very unlike the devoted vehicle enthusiast that she was. Out of the corner of her eye Paula watched in horror as an eighteen-wheel truck came barreling into the intersection, against the light.

"Cookie, look out!" Paula screamed.

Everything was happening so fast, yet somehow things seemed to move in slow motion. The truck moved steadily forward until it was almost directly in their path. Paula heard the blast of the truck's air horn, saw the driver leaning out of the window, red-faced, yelling something at them that she couldn't hear through the noise.

Cookie snapped to attention. Her hands tightened on the wheel, and her teeth were clenched in concentration.

Still, a crash seemed inevitable. A strange detached thought flashed through Paula's mind. I'm glad we buckled up for safety.

The car lurched as Cookie swerved sharply. Then there was an awful screeching sound as she hit the brake.

Chapter 8

That was a close one, Paula said silently to the reflection in her dressing table mirror that Saturday evening. It was some kind of miracle that Cookie managed to avoid hitting the truck. The car wasn't even scratched.

That truck driver was pretty mad, in spite of the fact that it was really his fault. Maybe next time he'd watch where he was going. She smiled — what were those words he'd been mouthing? If they were anywhere near as bad as what I heard Cookie shouting back. . . .

She opened her jewelry box. I wonder what Coralynn will be wearing, she thought, toying with an earring.

I wish I could stop feeling apprehensive about tonight. Maybe there really is something wrong with me. Even Mom said I seemed a little jumpy before she went away. She peered deeply into the eyes in the mirror.

Well, I'm not going to find the answer by staring back at myself, she thought, giving her head an impatient little shake. I'm going to have to be careful around Garth. I don't want to look like a little fool, panting after him. It wouldn't be a nice way to act, either, especially since Coralynn has invited me to her party. Still . . .

Paula allowed herself a moment to indulge in a fantasy about Garth. She closed her eyes and created his image — tall, blond, dressed in that casual way of his — with that dreamy, faraway look in his eyes. He was leading her to the dance floor and taking her in his arms.

He tilted her chin up gently and leaned down, his face closer and closer. She could almost taste his lips on hers. . . .

Abruptly, a vision of Coralynn's face, distorted with rage, blotted out the happy vision. Her features loomed large and threatening behind Paula's eyes. She didn't look like the Ice Princess now. She looked like the Wicked Queen.

Paula jumped as the phone rang and startled her back to reality. It rang again before she reached her bedside table and answered it.

Maybe it's Mom, she thought.

"Hello?"

Silence.

"Hello?" she tried again. She knew someone was there — she could hear them breathing.

"Hello?" She gave it one more try before hanging up. Probably some kids, she thought. Still, she didn't like getting prank phone calls — especially when she was home alone.

Paula sighed. No more daydreaming, she told

herself firmly. She walked to her closet and stared. What does one wear to a party like this? she wondered, fingering garment after garment. This pink dress with the scoop neck? No — I'll look like I'm going to a fashion show with my mom. The green jersey? No — I'll look like a Girl Scout. What would Cookie wear?

In this closet, nothing, she thought dismally. How can I expect Garth — no, not Garth — some other guy — to notice me with this Little Miss Goody-Two-Shoes wardrobe?

Wait a minute. She remembered the white cashmere sweater that almost came off the shoulder. She'd been saving it for the right moment. She ran to her bureau. Yes! she thought with excitement. This will seem sort of sophisticated — with my black jeans and those short suede boots.

Now I have to decide what jewelry to wear. She held the sweater out in front of her, trying to decide what would set it off.

The phone rang again. This time she deliberately let it ring two more times before picking it up.

"Hello?"

Again, there was silence on the other end. Paula was getting annoyed.

"Hello? Look, this isn't funny. . . . Do you have the wrong number or something?"

"No — I've got your number all right," came the answer. The voice sounded muffled and fuzzy. "You're not a good waitress, Paula. I've been trying to get your attention, but you just refuse to notice me. Pretty soon I'll have to do something drastic."

Paula slammed the phone down hard. "Pranksters!" she muttered angrily . . . but she wasn't entirely convinced.

She tried to put the call out of her mind as she continued to get ready for the party. But she felt edgy and was conscious of sounds in the empty house she hadn't noticed before, like the ticking of the clock and the hissing of the steam heat. She was eager to get out of there. Finally, she was ready to go.

Okay, she thought, gazing at her reflection in the mirror. Her hair flowed in shining waves over her shoulders; the sweater and jeans set off her slender figure. That's no Girl Scout, she told herself.

Darn! There was that phone again. She reached the table in two quick steps and grabbed the receiver.

"Leave me alone!" she said furiously.

"Huh? Hey, wait a minute." There was a smooth, masculine voice on the other end. "Is this Paula McLaughlin's residence?"

"Oh — ah — yes, this is Paula."

"Hi, Paula, this is Garth. Is something wrong?"

"I'm sorry — I've been getting some prank phone calls." And do I feel *foolish*, she felt like adding. What a surprise this is, she thought.

"Oh, I hate those. It's a really childish thing to do. Anyway — I just wanted to see if you decided to accept Coralynn's invitation. If you haven't, I'd like to talk you into coming to the party."

"As a matter of fact, I did."

"That's great, I'm glad I'll see you there." There

was a moment of uncomfortable silence, then Garth added, "I'd like to ask you if you wanted a ride — but my car is in the shop. I guess this phone call is a little unusual — but I'm glad I'll see you later."

Paula felt pleased but awkward. "I was just getting dressed."

"Oh. I'll let you go then. 'Bye."

" 'Bye." Paula hung up.

Idiot! she thought immediately. Why didn't you offer to give *him* a ride to the party? Now he probably thinks you were trying to get rid of him. Well — nothing you can do about that now, but try to do something about it later.

Still, the call had put a special sparkle into the evening. She picked up the pink lipstick she usually wore, then set it down again. Tonight I'm going to be different, she thought, picking up a red lipstick she had bought a while ago but never had the nerve to wear. Yes, this will be perfect for tonight, she said to herself, carefully applying the deep, almost blood-red color to her lips.

Chapter 9

Taking a deep breath, Paula pushed open the door of the Dog House and stepped inside.

The place had been transformed for Coralynn's party. Colored filters continuously faded the lighting from deep red to a pink and back again.

Paula threaded her way through the crowd, smiling and nodding. She breathed a sigh of relief as she noticed what the other guests were wearing. At least I'm dressed for the occasion, she thought. The closer she got to the dance floor, the more she could feel the music vibrate through her body. A band was playing in the far corner of the room, blasting out a thumping rock beat. Couples were packed tightly together, gyrating on the dance floor.

Loud, Paula said to herself. Well — it's great for dancing. And as long as I stay near the band, I won't have to worry about what to say — nobody could hear me anyway.

The band announced a short break, and Paula headed for the refreshment stand.

A guy dressed up in a bat costume with huge

bat wings and a bat mask leaned against the refreshment table. As Paula approached he began strumming the air as if he were playing a guitar, singing off-key, "You can see you've driven me batty, I've gone simply batty over you. But though I've gone batty, you still treat me ratty . . ."

A few of the guests chuckled. There's one in every crowd, Paula thought, and smiled.

The bat raised his mask and smiled back.

"Remember me?" he asked.

"Sure," Paula answered, thinking, he's Jimmy something-or-other from biology class. He was always doing something off the wall, trying to attract attention.

"Try the punch?" Jimmy offered

Paula nodded and picked up a glass. The punch bowl is crystal, she realized, staring. It's just like that dream I had, when I blacked out in gym class.

The music started up again. Paula smiled her good-byes to Jimmy, the class clown, and continued her search for the hostess. She finally spotted Coralynn's pale blonde hair. She was over near the bandstand, and Paula hurried to say hello.

As she tapped her on the shoulder, Coralynn spun around, her prepared welcoming smile frozen in place. Coralynn was saying something Paula couldn't understand, because the music was blaring so loudly. Something about "you're here."

"Yes, I just got here — I'm not late, am I?" she replied, taking a chance that Coralynn had just asked when she arrived. Then Coralynn said something else she didn't get — all she understood was "who" and "do." Who do you know? Who do you want to meet?

"I don't know many people here — but don't go to any trouble, I'll be okay," she answered, hoping that made sense.

But Coralynn's smile was growing icier by the minute. The song finished, and in the silence before the next one started Coralynn yelled, "I *said* who do you think you are!" A lot of people turned to see what was going on. Paula caught a glimpse of Cookie on the edge of the crowd.

Coralynn stared at Paula as they walked toward the door, followed by a little entourage of Coralynn's friends. As they got near the door, it was quieter. Coralynn faced Paula angrily.

"First you scald me, then accuse me of knocking you down, and we both know you've been trying to steal my boyfriend. How did you ever have the nerve to crash my party? I guess you knew Garth would be here so you just didn't care what you did. Well, you're not going to get away with it. He's *my* date. You're going to get out now, before he gets here."

Paula was speechless for a moment. "But you invited me!" she said finally.

Coralynn shook her head in disbelief. "What a ridiculous lie. Maybe that bump you got on the head — when you tripped over your own feet and fell down — really scrambled your brains. Look, here's your hat, what's your hurry, if you know what I mean. There's the door."

Coralynn walked away with a final contemptuous

backward glance. "Oh, and by the way, don't think I don't know who's been playing those little pranks on my aunt's customers. It's pretty obvious because nothing happened before *you* arrived."

She left Paula standing by the door. Coralynn's friends followed obediently behind her, shaking their heads disapprovingly in unison.

Idiot, Paula said to herself, feeling foolish. It was all a setup to embarrass me. It looks as if even Cookie was in on it — she didn't exactly rush to my defense. So, they had a little plan to make me look like a party crasher — it took me long enough to catch on.

Paula walked slowly outside, feeling alternately dejected and angry. Almost a full moon, she noticed. She hugged herself for warmth in the damp night air. Funny, she thought as she looked around the parking lot, this place doesn't look so spooky in the daytime — except for that mad dog on the sign.

The moon shone through the trees, giving off an icy silvery light Paula thought reminded her of something — something eerie. The parking lot seemed so quiet and empty, far away from the lights across the road. Why did I have to park my car around the back, next to the woods, she asked herself uneasily.

Suddenly she heard a crunching sound coming from somewhere behind the trees.

Was someone there?

Then she heard a scraping sound and looked in the direction of the noise — but she couldn't see anything.

45

Probably some animal — a squirrel or something, she decided, beginning to walk to her car. Who knows? she thought. I'm feeling so spooked I might have even imagined the noise.

Click. Click. Crunch, crunch, crunch, crunch.

That's not my imagination.

There was no mistaking the sound this time. It was footsteps. They weren't coming from the woods anymore — they had reached the asphalt of the parking lot.

CRUNCHCRUNCHCRUNCHCRUNCH . . .

The footsteps were louder, now . . . coming closer, coming faster. They were heading straight toward her.

Paula began walking faster and faster, then running with the footsteps in pursuit. She reached her car and fumbled for her keys. Her hands were shaking so hard, she kept missing the lock.

Even if I scream, no one would hear me over that music, she knew. She was still trying desperately to stop shaking enough to place the key in the lock, when arms gripped her from behind, and a hand closed over hers, pulling the key from her grasp.

Chapter 10

Suddenly Paula's terror was overcome by a flash of rage. She brought her elbow back hard, catching her captor sharply in the ribs. She felt him release his grasp and groan as she connected.

"*Uuuuh*," she heard him gasp as he staggered back. Paula spun around, searching for the keys she heard drop. Her eyes widened in horror as she recognized her pursuer.

"Oh, Garth! Oh, no, I'm so sorry." She ran to him and then stopped, unsure what to do next. Garth waved her off.

"It's okay, it's okay," he said weakly. He leaned against the car, clutching at his side.

"I heard footsteps, and I couldn't see who it was . . . I thought somebody was chasing me," she babbled.

"I — like I told you — my car is in the shop. I walked, and I took a shortcut through the woods — and then I saw you," he grunted.

"You were shaking like crazy," he said, straightening up carefully. He took a deep breath. "Whew! You've got a mean right!"

"Oh, gosh, I'm really sorry," Paula said again. "I wish there were something I could do."

"It's okay, I'll live," Garth replied, a little unsteadily. "Just don't let it get around that you almost knocked me out, okay?"

"Promise." Paula smiled.

"So what happened — aren't you going to the party, Paula?"

"No, no — I've already been."

"Hmm, my detective powers tell me something went wrong. Come on, let's go for a ride and you can tell me about it. By the way, mind if I drive?" Garth held out his hand for the keys. "You seem a little jumpy right now. Why don't we stop off someplace and have a soda or something?"

"Well, but what about your date?" Paula glanced back toward the Dog House.

"Listen, I don't have a date, and I never had a date for tonight. I was just going to the party, that's all. I can always come back later. Please?" he said, holding out his hand for the keys again.

Moments later they were on the road. Paula settled her head back against the seat. Is this a terrific coincidence — or a big mistake? she wondered.

Later, they were seated opposite each other in a booth at Scoop's ice-cream parlor. Garth ordered a coffee milk shake.

"I'll just have a Coke. I guess I'm not in an ice cream kind of mood," Paula murmured.

"Okay — I want you to tell me exactly what happened back there at the party." Garth placed his hand over Paula's.

For a moment Paula's mind was a blank. All she could think of was the way his hand felt on hers.

"Well, come on, it can't be that bad," Garth prompted, squeezing her hand tighter.

Please, don't let me start blushing, Paula prayed — but her face felt hot. She stared at the table, and then took a deep breath.

"Coralynn accused me of crashing her party in front of everyone." Paula told Garth about hitting her head in gym and blacking out. "Coralynn says it made me imagine she invited me — although I think she said it just to be sarcastic. I mean, it doesn't sound possible, does it?"

"Oh, come on, I don't think so," Garth said darkly. "Anyway — Coralynn could have made you feel welcome no matter what. You're new in town, and it's the decent thing to do. But what she did was — lousy." His eyes flashed angrily.

A voice behind them echoed, "Lousy."

Garth and Paula turned to see Coralynn standing there, with a few of her hangers-on.

"I'll tell you what *I* think is lousy." Coralynn's eyes blazed. "You're supposed to be at my party, with me, and I find you sneaking around with *her*! How dare you stand me up!"

If looks could kill . . . thought Paula. Without waiting for an answer Coralynn turned and walked away from the stunned couple, slamming the door behind her and her little group. The resounding *bang* as the door shut made the glass rattle.

"Spoiled brat," Garth muttered. He removed his hand from Paula's and raked it through his hair. "This is ridiculous — I just don't believe it," he murmured in exasperation.

Paula stared at the table, moving her soda glass back and forth. "Coralynn certainly seems to think you had a date with her," she said softly.

"But I *didn't*," Garth insisted. "Look, Paula, it's crazy. Coralynn and I hung out with the same crowd for years. She never showed any particular interest in me until this year, when out of the blue she asked me to go out.

"Okay, that's fine," he continued. "As a matter of fact, I liked the way she came right out and showed she liked me. We went out and had a nice time, and so I took her out again. That was the day you started working at the Dog House. That was our second date. After that, I don't know." Garth looked confused.

"She started telling me that 'we' had plans to do this or that, when I hadn't made any plans. I didn't like the way she started taking charge of me, questioning me, and following me around. She even started asking my friends questions about me — crazy questions.

"I didn't want to hurt her feelings, so I tried to tell her nicely that I thought we should just be friends. She said she agreed with me — so I decided to go to her party . . . and this is the first I've heard about a date. Honest, it is. I'm going to talk to Coralynn and get this whole thing cleared up."

Paula was quiet for a minute, letting the words sink in. Garth looked awfully sincere. "Well — I know Coralynn can be persistent," she said finally.

"Right," Garth agreed. "This is all some terrible misunderstanding. Anyway, I'd never make a date and just not show up. One thing you should know about me is that I'm a real gentleman." He grinned.

"A quality that's obviously appreciated by more than one girl," Paula teased, smiling mischievously. Then another thought occurred to her. She glanced around the crowded ice-cream parlor. "Say, Garth — if this place and the Dog House are the only places in town to go, why did that drive-in close? Was the food really awful? It looks like it was a nice place."

Garth sat up stiffly. "There was an accident," he mumbled. "Hey — I don't want to talk about something gruesome," he said suddenly, flashing that grin Paula found so irresistible. "I want to convince you that I'm a real *fun* guy. Besides, right now I want to talk about *you*."

"Okay, okay, you've convinced me." Paula smiled back.

You certainly are a fun guy, Garth Zvecker, she said to herself.

You're fun, and good-looking, and sweet, and sexy . . .

. . . and I bet you're hiding something.

Chapter 11

Paula floated down the hallway on her way to homeroom Monday morning. She glanced around at the faces, hoping she'd run into Garth. She'd been daydreaming about him since Saturday night.

What a good listener he is, Paula thought. Some guys only pretend to be listening, but I can feel Garth really concentrating on what I'm saying and trying to understand what I mean. She smiled as she remembered how he had taken her hand.

Uh-oh, she thought, catching sight of a little group. There's the welcoming committee. About halfway down the hall, under the big clock, stood Coralynn, surrounded by some of her friends.

For a moment Paula considered turning down one of the side corridors off the main hallway to avoid the confrontation that was sure to come.

No! she said angrily to herself. I'm not afraid of her, and she's not going to think she can make me run.

"Hey, look who's here!" Coralynn called as Paula grew nearer. "I want to talk to you — right now!"

"Well, I don't want to talk to *you*." Paula steadied herself, preparing to pass them by. But Coralynn and her girlfriends formed a little circle around her.

"So, you were planning on moving in on more than just my party, I see. Trying to steal my boyfriend isn't a smart thing to do — not smart at all." Coralynn's voice was quiet, and she stared steadily at Paula with a steely gaze.

"Get out of my way, Coralynn," Paula ordered firmly. She tried to move past again, but Coralynn stepped in front of her. She was shaking with rage, and looked almost completely out of control. For a moment Paula thought Coralynn might try to hit her or push her — but instead she opened her mouth and hissed, "Floozie!"

Paula heard a delicate chuckle behind her and recognized Virgilia's chirping voice. "Well, well, sticks and stones can break your bones but Coralynn's words can't hurt you. What a performance, Coralynn."

"Mind your own business, Little Miss Bookworm," Coralynn snapped. "This is *private*."

Virgilia smiled and shook her head in mock confusion. "Gee, I didn't know that. I didn't think anyone would discuss *private* business in a crowded hallway.

"By the way — I heard what happened at the party, and if lying makes your nose grow you're going to be paying my mom a visit real soon. Excuse us — uh — ladies."

Virgilia grinned as they walked away from a red-faced Coralynn. "My mom is a plastic surgeon —

nose jobs and all. Most people know that. I usually don't approve of being so nasty, but Coralynn is such a . . . *rat*. I heard what happened at the party."

"She's a rat, all right," Paula agreed. She paused as Virgilia stopped to retrieve a computer disc that had fallen out of her book bag. "You do your homework on computer discs?" Paula blurted out, surprised.

"Oh, no — not generally — just this big project I'm working on," Virgilia replied offhandedly as she straightened up.

Cookie walked by, heading in the opposite direction, and gave them both a big hello as she passed. Virgilia waved back, but Paula pretended not to notice. "News travels so fast around here — I guess everyone thinks I crashed Coralynn's party," she murmured to Virgilia.

"Not everybody pays so much attention to what Coralynn says," Virgilia replied. "I don't, for instance. And anyway, I wouldn't even want to be invited to a party with that bunch — just look at them," she said, glancing over her shoulder at Coralynn and her friends.

Sure enough, the group was nodding vigorously at Coralynn, who seemed to be running off at the mouth. They look like those little dolls that have springs for necks so their heads bob up and down, Paula thought.

Later on, in English class, she thought about what Virgilia had said. She certainly sounded as if she meant it — but still, didn't she mind at all that she wasn't invited to any of Coralynn's parties? Not even a little bit? They were huge social events.

"I'd like you to hand in your essay question assignments," Mr. Woods was saying. As Paula passed her paper forward, a warning bell began to sound in her brain. The fact that she had checked the assignment with Coralynn made her feel apprehensive.

Paula held her breath as she watched Mr. Woods flip through the stack of papers. He lingered over one, looking puzzled at first, then impatient.

"I see you decided to ignore my instructions and answered a question of your own choosing, Miss McLaughlin. You should try being a little less independent. That will be a grade of zero."

Paula knew Coralynn's face wore a smirk of satisfaction without having to turn around. Virgilia's comment popped into her mind. Yes, she's a rat all right, she thought with disgust.

She approached Mr. Woods cautiously after class. "Excuse me — I'd like to explain about the assignment." There was an uncomfortable silence as Mr. Woods didn't look up from the papers he was gathering.

"I checked the assignment with someone — and — well, they gave me the wrong information. Maybe they made a mistake and forgot to tell me."

Mr. Woods peered at her over his glasses. "Maybe next time you'll take care of your own responsibilities, instead of leaving it to someone else."

That's not fair, Paula thought, but aloud she said, "Yes, I'll be more careful. Is there any way to make up the assignment?"

"Well, you could bring in the correct assignment, completed, and the answer to an additional essay question, and give it to me on Thursday morning. Then I'd think about it."

"Thursday!" Paula wailed in panic. "That's no time at all. I have to work after school. I can't get any time off with such short notice — what can I do?"

"Do as you please, it's what you've been doing all along," said Mr. Woods breezily. Then he snapped his briefcase shut and was gone out the door.

Paula stared after him for a moment, feeling tired and defeated. Slowly she gathered her books and trudged toward the gym.

She recalled an old saying that a rather mean aunt of hers was fond of repeating, "Things always get worse before they get better."

I hope it's not true, she prayed.

Chapter 12

After Monday's hallway incident Coralynn stayed away from Paula, and Paula did her best to avoid Coralynn as well. By Wednesday she had finished most of the essay question assignment.

I'll finish the rest of it tonight after work, she thought as she walked into the gym for Dancercise class. She found a spot as far away from Coralynn as possible and began doing some warm-up stretches.

Thank goodness Trixie didn't need me yesterday, I got lots of work done, she thought as she warmed up. I'm not going to think about anything unpleasant during this class, she told herself. Not the paper, and not Coralynn.

"Class! I have an announcement to make, so listen up." Ms. Christiansen glanced at her watch. "Something has come up, and I'm going to have to leave right now. As you know, in a situation like this the class would usually be cancelled."

The class groaned in unison. This was a class everyone actually liked, and the girls all liked Ms.

Christiansen. She was so pretty and trim, and she always made the class so much fun.

"Hold on, everybody, hold on, I'm not finished." The teacher held up her hand for silence. "Today I've decided to try something different. A few of you seem to know the routines thoroughly and perform them very well, so I'm going to select one of those students to lead the class in my absence."

The girls waited expectantly. Out of the corner of her eye Paula saw Coralynn straighten up and smile, looking quite pleased with herself. Incredible, she thought to herself.

"Paula, I'd like you to take over. Don't worry if you don't remember every single thing, just do your best and I'm sure you'll be fine. Everybody, give Paula your full cooperation." She looked pointedly at Coralynn, who seemed caught so completely off-guard she looked rather comical.

With a determined effort not to be nervous, Paula stepped in front of the room. For the next forty minutes she was completely absorbed in concentration and physical exertion. She was so intent on her work that she got her wish — there was no room in her mind for thoughts of Mr. Woods, the paper, Coralynn, Garth, or any of her other daydreams.

Before she knew it, she was leading the class in the closing movements. "Right arm over . . . and left arm over . . . breathe deeply . . . again . . . and that's it! Thanks, everybody!" She grinned, feeling suddenly self-conscious.

"Way to go, Paula! Great job!" Students murmured words of congratulation as they filed out.

Coralynn had left early, she noticed. Cookie hadn't made it to class at all.

Paula turned off the stereo and placed the music tape on the shelf beside it. Then she checked the room to make sure it was neat and no one had left anything behind. At least there's something to be glad about today after all, she thought gratefully. Then she saw Garth standing just outside the doorway.

"We got off the field early, and I happened to glance in the rooms as I walked by, and I saw you leading the class. You were terrific!" he said enthusiastically.

Paula blushed. "I like to dance."

"You know," Garth went on, "they'll be holding auditions for the Spring Musical soon. It's usually pretty good, actually. You ought to try out."

"Oh, come on, Garth. I mean, thanks, but I haven't had any acting or dance training. Sure, it's nice to think about, but — "

"That kind of attitude will keep you doing just that — thinking about it. What if I just thought about football instead of playing?"

He gazed up at the ceiling. "I'm dreaming of running down the field and making a touchdown, ta-da!"

"Well, you won't get dirty," Paula quipped.

"I won't have any fun." He placed his hands on her shoulders and looked into her eyes.

"Okay, okay, I get the point. Maybe I will audition," she said after a moment. "Shoot! I'll be late for work — see ya!" She ran into the locker room, still feeling the warmth of his hands on her shoulders.

At the entrance to the locker room she stopped abruptly. What in the world is going on here? Strange — the last person out must have turned off the lights.

At least the shower room light is on, Paula sighed with relief as she moved cautiously through the banks of lockers. The showers stood at the end of the rows. The light glowed through a cloud of steam. She heard the hiss of running water.

"Anybody here?" she called. "Hey, anybody?" She felt her way along, wishing her eyes would hurry up and adjust to the dimness.

"Ow!" She bumped her head on an open locker door. "Darn it, why does mine have to be all the way in the back," she mumbled aloud, just to hear the sound of a human voice.

Then she heard loud crashing sounds. Someone was banging doors — they were banging them hard, one after the other, faster and faster. The noise was violent, and somehow threatening. Paula stood still, her hand over her heart.

Finally the banging stopped, and she heard the sound of running feet exiting the back way as the racket died out.

Still Paula stood there, her back pinned against a wall. She didn't know how much time had passed, when suddenly she remembered that she was supposed to be going to work.

Great — what time is it? She peered at the illuminated dial of her watch nervously. I should have been there by now! she thought, panicking.

Clenching her fists at her side she moved stiffly to the last row of lockers, the ones just opposite the shower lanes.

Why is my locker door open? she thought, for a moment feeling only puzzled. Then fear prickled the hair on the back of her neck. Her belongings formed a trail from one end of the shower lane to the next. Soggy books and papers were strewn about. Her handbag was soaking in a puddle of water, and she found her keys in another puddle nearby.

So this is why they left the shower on, she thought, gazing sadly at the devastation.

Then she saw the tattered mess of her waitress uniform. It was lying in the far corner of the stall. As she picked up the ruined mess she saw that it wasn't just torn — someone had slashed up and down the front with something red — probably a lipstick. Through the glistening water in the steamy light, the lipstick looked like blood.

Chapter 13

It took Paula some time to straighten out her things. It was nearly an hour before she rushed into the Dog House, still wearing her gym suit under her coat.

"Hello, Trixie, I'm sorry I'm late — " she began breathlessly. "I tried to call but — "

"Thanks for doing me a favor and showing up at all," Trixie said sarcastically, cutting her short.

Tardiness was Trixie's pet peeve. Paula took a deep breath and tried again.

"I'm sorry, I really couldn't help it. Listen, something happened to my uniform — do you have a spare one downstairs? I've got my apron and shoes here."

"I'm sure you had better things to do over at the high school than worry about a little thing like this job. I ought to get some professional waitresses who don't think this job is a big joke," Trixie steamed on. Then she turned and started walking away, leaving Paula standing there feeling extremely foolish.

Trixie turned around again, and Paula breathed a sigh of relief as the scowl gave way to a red-lipped smile. "Okay, okay, there's a spare uniform downstairs — but get back up here on the double. It's hanging on the end hook."

Paula raced down the stairs feeling sad, and soggy. Her coat had a damp spot on the side from the wet books and clothes she had carried.

I hate it down here, she thought, gazing at the unshaded light bulb as she dressed quickly. She was reaching for her apron when she heard someone clumping down the stairs.

"Is that you, Cookie? Virgilia?" she called.

"Sorry, sweetie, it's only me," Coralynn said, sitting down on a bench with a grimace. She pulled off her shoes and began massaging her feet slowly. "Aunt Trixie made me waitress since you were late," she whined. "Well, maybe I have to help out but she's not going to make a waitress out of me. That's *your* job."

"Well, I wonder who's fault it was that I was late," Paula snapped accusingly.

"Oh, please don't try to blame *me*," Coralynn said with a sneer.

Paula gave an exasperated sigh and began tying her apron.

"You'd better find your own boyfriend, too, if you know what's good for you," Coralynn hissed. "I don't mind playing rough." As she turned her blonde hair swung out so that just the edge brushed Paula's cheek. "Chicken?" she asked as she started climbing quickly up the stairs.

How can anyone be so nasty all the time? Paula asked herself as she tied the apron on and marched upstairs. She paused at the entrance to the dining room. The place was packed. She remembered the way Trixie described it when it was like this — "a madhouse, just a madhouse."

She certainly was right. Paula headed in the direction of the waitress station to pick up some checks and menus. That's when she saw Garth — leaning back casually in his seat — next to Coralynn!

No wonder Coralynn was in such a hurry to get upstairs, she thought, feeling a wave of disappointment.

What is he doing there?

Is this part of some kind of joke Garth and Coralynn are playing on me?

No — it can't be. But if it isn't, why is he sitting there with her?

Chapter 14

Trixie poked her red head out of the kitchen. "Come on, let's go. Don't just stand there admiring the view — help get these orders out!"

Why is everybody picking on me? Paula wondered, beginning to feel sorry for herself.

"Hey, I was afraid something happened to you! Tell me later, you know, why you were late," Cookie said, smiling cheerily.

"I'm fine," Paula said tightly and hurried away. Hands were waving for service everywhere.

"Hey, please, I'm starving," a big guy pleaded as she passed. She recognized him as one of the guys on the football team.

"Okay," Paula said breathlessly. "What'll it be?" Holding her pad in one hand she fumbled in her apron pocket for a pen.

"Uh — do you have butterscotch pudding?"

"No," she continued searching, "just rice pudding."

"Oh. Well, do you have tutti-frutti ice cream?"

"No, no — just what's on the menu."

"Oh. Well, I guess you don't have any lime Jell-O then, either."

Paula shook her head no. Where was that darn pen, anyway?

"Okay — then I'll just have the fish sandwich — and some french fries, a Coke and — "

"Oh!" Paula gasped in surprise. She had felt a sharp, stinging sensation and jerked her hand out of her apron pocket. At the sight of blood on her fingers, she drew in her breath again quickly and stared in horror.

The beefy guy jumped out of the booth. "Shhhh! Easy, easy," he said gently taking her hand and examining it. "Look — look, it's just a scratch. You were so surprised you pulled your hand away before you got hurt too bad . . . by whatever it was." Paula glanced around. Apparently, nobody at any of the other tables had noticed.

Paula untied her apron and dumped the contents on the table. Pens, checks, a rubber band, a couple of paper clips . . . and a knife. It was a sharp one — a steak knife. They didn't use those very often.

"Wow," said the big guy. "It's a good thing you didn't get a bad cut."

"Well, you were right, it's just a scratch," Paula told him. "I was more surprised and scared than hurt, but I've got to put something on this just in case. I'll come back as fast as I can and take your order."

"Hey, that's okay." He put a big hand to his stomach. "I'm not too hungry anymore — I think I'll leave. I hate the sight of blood."

Paula washed her hands and applied a Band-Aid from the first aid kit. Playing pranks was one thing — but knives were dangerous. She shuddered to imagine what could have happened.

Moments later she walked into the kitchen to tell Trixie about it. "Somebody put a knife in my apron pocket — " she began. Trixie was grilling hamburgers.

"Bet I know just who it was, too." Trixie didn't miss a flip. "You get hurt bad?"

"No — scratched — but I could have. So — you think you know who did it?" she said in surprise. Would Trixie really suspect Coralynn — her own niece?

"Yes, I do for a fact. You."

"ME!"

"Uh-huh. And here's how it happened 'cause I've seen it lots of times before. Even did it once myself. You were busy, you were thinking of eighteen things at once. You got to the table with the silverware and you found you had an extra steak knife — so you dropped it in your pocket. You meant to put it back and you didn't.

"That was the last table you waited on that night, and then you hung up the apron and forgot about it. Are you okay to work?"

"Sure, I guess so," Paula said weakly. Trixie sounded so sure . . . was it possible that it happened just as she said it did? Of course it was — it gets busy sometimes, and it's hard enough to remember from one minute to the next, Paula decided.

"Remember — I said that carelessness was one

of the main ways accidents happen," Trixie continued. "I know it's not easy, but you've got to be watching every single minute — no matter how busy you are."

"Right. I'll be more careful." Paula headed back out to the roaring dining room.

"Hi!" chirped Virgilia. "Boy, am I glad to see you. Can you give me a hand taking some of these orders out? Uh — that one's for Coralynn's table — sorry, I'm swamped." Virgilia was piling dishes on a tray that looked bigger than she was.

"It's okay, I can stand it." Paula grabbed the dish — a covered plate.

A covered dish — that's odd — I didn't think we served anything in a covered dish, she thought absently as she carried it away.

"I've been waiting," Coralynn drawled, as Paula knew she would. She was determined not to let Garth — or Coralynn — know how upset she was at seeing them sitting together.

"Madame is served." She placed the dish in front of Coralynn and removed the cover, saying, "Ta-da!"

Ta-da indeed. Everyone stared in horror at what was on Coralynn's plate . . . a big, fat, dead, long-tailed — RAT!

. . . But wait . . . dead?

No . . . the rat was moving.

Chapter 15

The rat on Coralynn's plate seemed to be in its final death throes. As Coralynn and Garth stared in surprise and horror Paula slammed the lid back on the dish, covering the hideous thing. Garth was looking a little green, Paula could see.

Anyone who wasn't alerted by the crash of the lid soon knew something terrible had happened because Coralynn let out a shriek that could wake the dead. As the crowd gathered she turned to Paula.

"How *could* you? Oh, it's so terrible."

This is familiar, Paula thought, recalling her first day working at the Dog House. Coralynn had pointed the finger at her then, too, and she'd been too shocked, too timid, and too embarrassed to say anything in her own defense. This time, she decided, things were going to be different.

"Listen, Coralynn, I wouldn't handle a dead rat no matter how much I disliked someone."

But I *did* handle it, in a way, when I carried the dish over here. Paula steadied herself against a wave of nausea as this thought occurred to her.

The word *rat* seemed to ricochet through the crowd. There were cries of "awful," "sickening," "horrible," and sounds of disgust.

Customers were leaving without bothering to pay their checks. In fact, quite a few were racing for the door. Trixie could spot a walkout a mile away, and she burst out of the kitchen like a shot.

"You get right back in here and pay those bills. What's the matter, has everybody gone stark raving mad?"

Trixie trotted over to the table, where a few of the more hearty and curious were demanding to see the rat. "Awww, c'mon, guys, just give us a look."

"Well, what's everybody staring at?" said Trixie, making a move to pull the cover off the dish. This made Coralynn cower even further into the corner.

"I wouldn't do that, Trixie," Virgilia spoke up. "It's probably pretty unpleasant. Look, I'm not squeamish, and I'll be careful. I'll just take it right out to the garbage for you," she said, grabbing the covered dish firmly and heading through the kitchen to the garbage cans around the side.

"She put it on my plate!" Coralynn accused again, staring at Paula.

To Paula's surprise, Trixie said "Oh, hush up, Coralynn, hon. Paula wouldn't handle a dead rat any more than you or I would."

Trixie gazed around sadly at the empty tables. "Well, I guess that's that," she said, and strode back to the kitchen.

"I'll take you home, Coralynn," Paula heard

Garth say as he slid out of the booth. Coralynn followed, glaring at Paula all the while.

Paula watched as they walked to the door together.

Well, as Trixie says, that's that, Paula sighed regretfully to herself. Some joke he played on me.

But as Garth got to the door Paula saw him motion Coralynn ahead. Then he began walking back to Paula. Quickly, she looked down and began cleaning the table.

"I've got to talk to you, Paula," Garth began. "I just want to take Coralynn home. She's had a bad shock . . . in more ways than one, and it's what I feel I should do. But I want to explain — I'll be right back. You'll be here?"

Paula didn't look up. "Okay," she said finally.

"Okay, then — I'll be right back." Garth trotted for the door.

Paula continued making the rounds from table to table, removing dishes and piling them on the bus trays, wiping off the tables. She found a few checks people had left and tucked them into her pocket.

A dead rat is sure going to improve business, she thought to herself.

As she was giving a last look around the dining room she heard Virgilia's voice behind her.

"Hey, Paula, check this out!"

Paula turned, and stared in disbelief. There was Virgilia, standing in the doorway, beaming, and holding the dead rat by the tail!

Smiling broadly, Virgilia began to sing. "M-I-C-K-E-Y M-O-U-S-E!"

Chapter 16

"It was only one of those toy novelty rats they sell to scare people, but it was so ugly and it looked so real," Paula told Garth later as they huddled against the chill on the steps behind the Dog House that night. "Virgilia showed me where the batteries were that made it move. She said she was suspicious from the moment she saw it — and she just had to check."

"Well, it sure scared me," Garth said, leaning back and staring up at the sky. "It was great timing, too. I already felt like a rat — Coralynn was angry because I didn't want to go out with her — you were angry because you thought I *did* . . ."

". . . and then the rat arrived," Paula finished for him.

"Right." Garth nodded. "I'm sorry you thought I double-crossed you."

"I'm sorry I jumped to conclusions. With everything that's been going on lately, it's getting hard to trust anybody. Look at this." Paula pulled a ketchup-stained check out of her pocket. "I found this on one of the tables."

Garth took the check and examined it. On it someone had written in red, *Better watch out or you'll have a bad accident.*

"Hmmm, the merry prankster again." He handed her back the check. "Well — it doesn't have your name on it. Maybe the message was meant for someone else."

"Well — I guess that's possible," Paula said slowly. "You know — I was sure it was Coralynn — but there's no way she'd put a rat on her own plate. Even Coralynn wouldn't go that far. I feel like someone is . . . toying with us."

"Wait a minute." Garth looked skeptical. "You know — I bet these things aren't all being done by one person. Maybe it's a few different people just blowing off steam — high school jitters and all."

"I'm not sure what you mean."

"Well, just think," Garth said hurriedly. "Our lives are changing so fast. One minute we were kids and the next we're adults making all kinds of decisions. People have a lot of adjusting to do. Maybe some are trying to find ways to deal with the pressure."

"I suppose when you put it that way, it makes sense," Paula said slowly. "I mean, I know I want to finish high school — graduate — and I'm planning to go to college, and then who knows what?"

"Yeah, I know," Garth said solemnly. "Graduation's a big deal, all right. I've had lots of good times here and that means leaving that behind. Still, I'm looking forward to it — it's exciting to look forward to having new experiences, trying new things and meeting new people — seeing what's out there."

Paula could feel his enthusiasm — it was catching. "You're right," she agreed. "And after graduation — no more being a waitress at the Dog House!" Her eyes sparkled. "And then maybe . . ."

She stopped as she saw Garth looking at her as his face moved closer to hers, and she closed her eyes. He kissed her softly and lightly at first, and then his kisses grew longer and more urgent.

Later they lingered in the darkness, holding each other. They thought they were alone, but while they were talking, kissing, someone else was hiding in the shadows . . . watching . . . listening. If they had seen that face they would have been scared — even terrified. For the face of the silent watcher was twisted into an expression of bitterness and hatred — and something else that could only be called madness.

Chapter 17

Paula could still feel the tingling warmth of Garth's kisses as she drove home later that night.

Perhaps that's why she didn't notice the first little knocking noises from the engine.

Later, as she drove further on, the noises grew louder. But by then she was absorbed in unraveling the mystery of who had been playing the pranks that were growing more and more dangerous.

Is Garth right? she wondered. Is it several people pulling random pranks? No crazed villain with an evil plan? Maybe.

But the rat — something about that bothers me. Virgilia said Coralynn was a rat — and it was Virgilia who asked me to take the rat to her table.

It was Virgilia who offered to take the rat away, too — she wasn't afraid. Could it be that she knew it was a fake all along — because she put it on the dish herself?

But why?

Did Virgilia want to get back at Coralynn for something — like not inviting her to all those parties — in spite of what she said? But then why drag me into it?

Paula couldn't think of a single reason Virgilia would want to hurt her — they seemed to get along fine. Besides, she didn't really want to believe it was Virgilia.

I can't picture Virgilia breaking into my gym locker and trashing my stuff, she thought, sighing in frustration. I guess that means I'm not one bit closer to figuring anything out.

The car had been slowing down, Paula realized. She stepped on the accelerator as she turned into Lonesome Lane.

Knock knock knock went the engine.

Drat! What's that noise, and how long has the car been doing that? She scolded herself for daydreaming while she was driving.

Now the car began to sputter and shake, lurching back and forth in a series of little spasms.

Oh, please — this is the worst possible place to break down, she thought, gazing at the bare trees on either side of the narrow strip of road. Their branches formed a canopy overhead.

It feels as if I'm miles away from anywhere, she thought, pumping the gas pedal. But no matter what she did, things got worse until the car finally stalled completely.

Great, she muttered, looking out at the empty woods. I'll get out of the car and a maniac will stagger out of the woods and carry me off, she thought grimly as she grabbed a flashlight.

At least the battery was working. Not that it

matters much, she said to herself as she raised the hood and peered into the engine. In the back of her mind she could hear her mother saying, "I told you so. I told you to take auto shop, but you wouldn't listen."

Okay, so you were right. Now what?

She shivered in the darkness, wondering whether to try to make it home — or go back the other way and try to phone from a gas station, when she heard the sound of an engine. Somebody's coming, let's just hope it's not some murderer, she prayed, listening carefully.

In a moment she could make out the form of a motorcycle driven by a familar figure. It's Cookie! she realized happily, forgetting about her grudge against Cookie for the moment.

The bike rumbled to a halt. Cookie removed her helmet. "Looks like you've got engine trouble. Can I help?" Cookie walked over to the car and peered under the hood.

"Sure." Paula handed her the flashlight.

"I can't tell what's wrong — we probably couldn't fix it out here anyway," Cookie said without looking up from the engine.

She stood up. "I can't tell what's wrong between us, either."

Paula looked at her. "You can't? What about Coralynn's party, Cookie? I saw you when she was claiming I crashed it. Why didn't you say something? You're the one who talked me into going — insisting Coralynn was okay. It seems a little strange."

Cookie stared back at Paula for a moment. "I don't know how you could expect me to hear what Coralynn was saying at that party. You know how loud the music was — I barely saw you. When I didn't see Garth for a while I thought maybe you both left. I didn't find out what happened until a few days later. By then you'd already been acting kind of funny, and I didn't put it together. I was going to ask you about it."

Of course. Paula remembered that she hadn't heard Coralynn right herself, at first, because the music was so loud. "So — you had nothing to do with it after all."

"No, silly," Cookie replied. "Hey — isn't it spooky out here?" She took Paula's arm. "Somebody died out here once. I can show you where."

"For heaven's sake — I don't want to go walking around these woods at night, looking for the place where somebody died!" Paula said with alarm, pulling her arm free.

"Okay, okay. I was only kidding, you know, trying to lighten up the situation. It was the first thing that came to mind. Sometimes my sense of humor is a little — different," Cookie said with a shrug.

"I'll say," Paula agreed.

"Anyway," Cookie said, "I vote that we get you home, so hop on. You can get the car towed tomorrow. Now — watch out because I don't have another helmet and this road is bumpy. I tend to drive kind of fast but I'm going to be careful, okay?"

"Uh — okay," Paula replied hesitantly. Didn't Cookie know how strange she sounded saying things like *I'll show you where somebody died*, and *I tend to drive kind of fast and this is a bumpy road*?

Well, I can't stay out here, so what else can I do besides "hop on," as she says? Paula thought.

The sight of approaching headlights brought Paula a wave of relief. Then a horn beeped and Trixie stuck her head out the window.

"Isn't it a little late for a pow-wow out here, ladies?"

"Car trouble," Paula explained. "Then Cookie came by and was about to give me a lift — but she doesn't have another helmet."

"Say, now, that's dangerous. It's a good thing I happened along. I'll drive you home."

"Thanks a lot," Paula said gratefully, walking around to the side of the car. She opened the door and was about to get in when she stopped and turned to Cookie. "Thanks for offering me the ride. And Cookie — I'm sorry — about the party, you know."

"Let's forget it," Cookie said with a wave of her hand. Paula saw her strap on the helmet as Trixie started up the car.

"Cookie's a good girl," Trixie said, smiling. "Reminds me a little bit of myself at that age. She knows how to have fun, and she's a darn good waitress. That's why I gave her a job right away after that other place she worked at closed — you know, that tacky little drive-in."

"The drive-in," Paula repeated. "Cookie used to work there? Nobody seems to want to talk about what happened there. Why?"

"Well — maybe nobody likes to remember," Trixie said, scowling now. "A guy from the high school died. Keeled right over onto his plate. But I, for one, don't think she had anything to do with it," she said firmly.

Paula's eyes widened. "That's terrible! W-what did he die of?" she asked, pointing to her house.

Trixie pulled the car into Paula's driveway. Then she turned and faced her. "Food poisoning," she said.

Chapter 18

What a night, Paula thought as she unlocked the
front door. Inside there were two messages waiting
for her on the answering machine. The first was an
extended message from her mother saying she'd be
delayed on business a few more days.

"Darn!" Paula muttered. Normally she liked it
when her mother was away on business. Sure, she
missed her, but she was glad for the chance to be
on her own and proud of the way it made her feel
adult and independent. However, with all the things
that had been going on, coming home to an empty
house was kind of creepy.

She chuckled to herself as her mother's message
ended with " . . . have a nice day, dear." Paula
started to hang up her coat as a pause and a beep
signaled the start of another message.

At the sound of the caller's voice Paula dropped
her coat to the floor and whirled around, pressing
her hand to her throat.

"Hello, Paula the waitress," the smooth teasing
voice began. "I was watching you tonight at the

restaurant. Now I have an order to give you — here it is. Go over to the window and stick your head out . . . *but* . . . and this is very important, Paula. *Do not open the window first!* That's an order. Get it? Hahahahahaha . . ."

Paula listened as the weird laughter trailed off. She knew that voice. She was almost certain that it was the same person who had called her on the night of Coralynn's party.

Whoever it was sounds really sick, she thought with a shudder. *They probably think they're very clever and are having a good laugh right now. I wonder if that part about being at the restaurant tonight was true? No,* she decided. *They probably just said that to scare me.*

With a final glance at the answering machine, Paula padded into the kitchen to make some tea. She selected her favorite, Red Zinger, and put the kettle on.

I hope working on Mr. Woods's essay question will help take my mind off some of the things that have been going on . . . but it's not likely, she thought.

She got her English book and some paper, sat down at the kitchen table, and started to work. She was scribbling a few notes when the loud whistling of the tea kettle made her jump out of her seat.

She laughed nervously to herself as she turned off the kettle. *Imagine me leaping up at the sound of the tea kettle,* she thought as she sat down again, feeling foolish. *I'm glad nobody was watching me.*

Just then there was a loud crash outside. Paula

glanced in the direction of the noise, which seemed to come from just outside the kitchen window. She sucked in her breath sharply.

Someone was watching her now. Two green eyes stared at her through the window.

It's that cat — the one I've seen around here a couple of times, she realized as she recovered from being startled. Honestly, my nerves are frazzled, she thought as she walked to the window and pushed it open.

"Here, kitty, kitty, kitty," she called.

The cat continued to stare at Paula, its back arched in fright. Slowly, Paula opened the window farther and called to it again. The cat hissed and then yowled as it jumped away, knocking over a garbage can.

Poor thing was scared to death, Paula thought. She closed the window and headed back to the table. I should be more careful — it could be sick and it could have scratched me, she scolded herself.

The sound of shattering glass made her turn. She was just in time to see a rock come crashing through the kitchen window. It landed on the spot where Paula had been standing moments before, sending fragments of glass into the sink and onto the floor.

A dog started barking, and the lights were switched on in old Mr. Tucker's house next door. "Hey! Stop that racket!" Mr. Tucker yelled from the second-story window.

Paula stood there in shock. Moments later Mr. Tucker appeared on the lawn, a staggering sight in red flannel pajamas, his long, wispy gray hair flying.

He began running across the lawn and into Paula's backyard, croaking, "Stop, you! Stop, you scoundrel!"

What can that old man be thinking? Paula wondered with alarm. Whoever threw that rock could hurt him.

Mr. Tucker ran out of sight. Slowly Paula began sweeping up the glass from the floor and cleaning it out of the sink. She nearly cut herself twice on tiny slivers.

She had swept up all the glass she could find and replaced the broom and dustpan when the front door bell rang. "Who is it?" she called as she stepped to the door.

"Open up!" an impatient voice she recognized as Mr. Tucker's barked. "I've caught the bum I saw skulking around in your backyard, making noise and waking up half the neighborhood. Come on, we'll get 'em inside and call the police!"

Cautiously, Paula opened the door and peered out at the red-faced Mr. Tucker, gripping the culprit by the arm.

"Garth!" she gasped.

Chapter 19

Somehow Paula managed to drag herself out of bed when the clock radio went off at five the next morning. She had set it extra early so that she'd have time to finish the essay questions that were due today. After everything that had happened the night before, it had taken her a long time to fall asleep.

Garth had told her and Mr. Tucker that he was out walking and had run into Cookie, who was on her way home. Cookie told him what had happened with Paula's car, and on impulse he had decided to come over and see if she had gotten home all right. When he reached her house he saw someone lurking around the backyard, but they got away before he could grab them. Then Mr. Tucker had grabbed *him*.

Mr. Tucker hadn't been convinced by this story, but Paula managed to talk him out of calling the police. Still, he insisted on watching while Garth walked to the end of the block and turned the corner. When he found out that Garth and Paula knew each other, he looked at her as if she were some sort of criminal. After he was satisfied that Garth was on his way home he turned to Paula and snarled, "You see what happens when you hang around with a bad element." Then he had stalked back home, looking disgusted.

Paula forced herself to banish Mr. Tucker from her thoughts and concentrate on the essays. By seven, she was finished. She took her mother's car, drove to school early, and deposited the paper on Mr. Woods's desk before he arrived.

It was a very, very long day.

How did I stay awake through all my classes? she wondered as she trudged down the hall at 3:15. She passed the drama office and decided to see if the scripts and dance audition requirements for the Spring Musical were ready. To her surprise, she saw Mr. Woods seated behind the desk, shuffling through some papers.

Oh, no — *he* is involved in it, she thought with a sinking heart. Then she marched toward the desk. I'm going to do it anyway, she told herself with determination.

"Excuse me, are the scripts for the Spring Musical ready — and . . ."

"Not yet," Mr. Woods cut her off, without looking up from his papers. "Keep checking, they'll be ready soon. When you get your copy, hang on to it — copies are so expensive, you know."

"Yes," she murmured and hesitated a moment before asking, "are you involved with the musical?"

"Why, yes — I always am. Of course, I'm only available for advisement. The students put it all together themselves." He looked up and his glance flickered over her face briefly before returning to his papers.

"Oh — well, thank you." Paula turned to leave the room. I'm still going to try, she told herself firmly as she walked toward her locker.

"Miss McLaughlin, Miss McLaughlin, wait a moment!" Paula heard behind her, and turned to see Mr. Woods scampering down the hall. "I didn't have a chance to tell you that I've read your essay answers and I think they're quite good. You managed to finish, I see."

"Yes," Paula replied quietly. I'm dead tired, too, since I had to get up at five o'clock this morning to do it, she wanted to add.

"Well, isn't it surprising what we can do when we set our minds to it?" he said as he adjusted his bow tie. His eyes twinkled as he looked at Paula, as if they shared a happy secret. "I don't know about you, but it certainly makes me feel good." He smiled and patted his lapels. Then he nodded politely and walked away.

Paula wanted to giggle. Mr. Woods looked so pleased she was afraid he might do a little dance. Still, she thought, he's not so bad after all — just eccentric.

Cookie walked by. "Hey, Paula, what's up?"

Paula shrugged. "Oh, not much, except I got about four hours' sleep, and I had to get my car towed to a garage — and — I'm too tired to go into it right now. How about you? You seemed a little — tense last night."

"Yeah, well, I was," Cookie agreed. "Remember I told you there was something I had to think through? Well — I have. I was thinking of dropping out of school. Trixie said she'd take me on as manager at the Dog House and train me."

"Cookie!"

"Relax, relax, I'm not going to do it." Cookie leaned against the wall. "I mean, you've got to grow up some time, right? I'll admit it's tempting, but it might not be what I want in the future, and I don't want to limit myself that way."

"Thank heavens."

Cookie lifted her shoulders. "Well, I'm glad, too. Now I just have to tell Trixie."

"Speaking of Trixie," Paula said hesitantly, playing with a lock of hair, "she mentioned that drive-in last night. She said a guy died there, and she also said you used to work there. You must have known — so why didn't you mention it when we drove by the place and I asked why it closed? Garth acts mysterious about the place, too."

Cookie sighed and shook her head. "Trixie's great, but she gossips like a kid. You see, Jeff — the guy that was killed, was kind of a jerk. He was always acting like a big shot, bragging about his college athletic scholarship and how it was going to get him out of this dump. He and his friends used to go all over town acting obnoxious, and that's what they were doing that day in the drive-in, and I had their table."

Cookie took a deep breath before she continued. "So I got into an argument with them about the way they were acting, and Garth was there and he jumped in. They started yelling at each other and it got pretty nasty, before the owner broke it up. Jeff and his friends hung around, though. About an hour or so later Jeff complained of stomach pains — soon after that he was dead. Some of Jeff's friends started a rumor that Garth and I had something to do with Jeff's death — but the police weren't convinced."

"I can see why it's not a popular topic of conversation for you or Garth," Paula said slowly. "But if he died from food poisoning, well, isn't that really an accident?"

Cookie frowned. "Trixie and her gossip — she always gets something turned around. It wasn't food poisoning. Someone put poison *in* the food."

Chapter 20

A wave of fatigue came over Paula after Cookie said good-bye and hurried to work. She felt relieved that she had the day off. The story about the restaurant gave her the creeps. The case was still under investigation, and if what Cookie had told her was true, then a killer was still out there somewhere.

It could be someone I see every single day, Paula thought as she watched the faces pass by in the hallway. She didn't like to consider the possibility.

Come on, snap out of it, she told herself. She remembered that she wanted to call the garage and find out what was wrong with her car, and headed over to the pay phone. Stifling a yawn she dropped a coin in the slot and dialed.

A mechanic answered on the third ring. He assured her that they'd found the cause of her car trouble.

"Your fuel line is gummed up pretty bad. Gonna cost you a couple hundred to fix it, and if you want us to go ahead and do the job you've got to leave it here for a few days."

"Do you know how it happened?"

"Oh, sure, lady, no doubt about it," the mechanic chuckled.

What's so funny? Paula thought impatiently.

"Somebody poured a whole lot of sugar in your gas tank — that's why the car stalled out."

There was another chuckle, but Paula was too startled to be annoyed. "What? Are you absolutely sure?"

The mechanic wasn't laughing anymore. "Of course I'm sure!" he barked. "Hey — if you don't think I know what I'm doing you can take your car somewhere else."

Paula held the receiver away from her ear until his yelling subsided. "Okay, okay, I was just surprised. I guess you might as well go ahead and fix it — I really need the car."

Paula hung up slowly. She felt as if events were closing in on her. So many strange things were happening, and none of them made any sense.

The idea that someone had deliberately sabotaged her car angered her, but it frightened her, too. She had an idea that whoever it was had something else in store for her.

May as well leave all my books at school, since I'm incapable of studying tonight, she told herself as she trudged toward her locker.

As usual, the lock was stubborn and it took her a few minutes to get the door open. She had finally succeeded when she heard a commotion at the other end of the hallway. She hesitated a moment, then locked the door and hurried to see what had happened.

Virgilia was standing in front of her open locker with a small cluster of students around her.

"Hey, Virgil, what is it?" Paula asked breathlessly.

Virgilia's face was deathly pale.

"My computer discs — everything from the research project I've been working on — they're gone! Do you know how much work that was?" she blurted out.

"Oh, no — that's terrible," Paula murmured. "Wait a minute. Are you sure you remember where you put them? Could they be at home — or in a classroom?"

Virgilia sighed and chewed on her lower lip. "I've been over it and over it. I put the discs in my book bag last night, but I didn't have time to do anything with them after I came home from work. The bag has been in my locker all day — the only thing I've taken out of it is my notebook. Those discs should still be in there."

"Well, maybe you should check around, just in case," Paula suggested.

Virgilia was growing more and more agitated. "You don't understand," she said hurriedly. "I don't lose things. The last time I misplaced anything was probably a Tinker Toy in nursery school!"

Coming from almost anyone else, a statement like that would sound strange and conceited. When Virgilia said it, it was just a fact, Paula realized. Virgilia was incredibly careful and precise.

Now Virgilia began twisting her hands. "Somebody broke into that locker and stole those discs," she said firmly. "Somebody who didn't want me to get my scholarship. I'm going to report this right now!"

She slammed the locker door and stormed down the hall.

The crowd began to disperse, but Paula remained a few moments. She had never seen Virgilia get rattled before.

Virgilia had slammed the locker door so hard it had popped open again, Paula noticed, and moved to shut it. She stopped at the sight of something inside.

Bugs!

There were dozens of them, all different sizes and colors, in clear plastic bags on the locker shelves. Paula stood gaping at them for a moment, and then took down a few bags to examine them.

There were plastic spiders and tarantulas, plastic worms, and even plastic flies.

What strange things, she thought, putting them back in the locker. Some of them look so real, too. What would somebody like Virgilia want with things like this — and where would she get them?

Then a thought dawned on her.

They were the kind of things you'd find in a novelty store.

The same kind of store where you could buy phony lizards and rubber snakes, or a fake, battery-powered, plastic rat!

Chapter 21

Was it Virgilia who had been playing the sick pranks all along? It seemed so unbelievable — and why would she do it, Paula wondered as she drove home. She had dismissed her fleeting suspicions about Virgilia, and she didn't like dredging them up again. Now she found herself trying to come up with new angles and possible motives.

But Paula was too worn out to continue that line of thinking for very long. She realized that her brain felt too numb. Moments after parking the car in the driveway she lay in her bed, sleeping soundly.

Paula didn't awaken until the following morning when the persistent ringing of the phone penetrated her consciousness. Then she lay there feeling groggy and disoriented, until she couldn't stand to listen to the noise any longer.

Reluctantly, she answered, "What is it?"

"Hi, you don't sound very cheery. I would have called you last night but I knew you were tired."

Paula sat up and smiled at the sound of Garth's voice. "Hi, what time is it anyway?"

"Seven-thirty."

"Wow! I slept for almost fourteen hours!"

"Was it all beauty sleep?" Garth laughed. "Anyway, do you want a lift to school?"

"Sure!" Paula agreed. "Mmmmm, that is if you don't mind bringing me back home this afternoon so I can take Mom's car to work tonight."

"No problem," Garth answered quickly. "I'd offer to give you a ride home from the Dog House later tonight, but I've got basketball practice after school, and then a load of homework. Anyway, shall I come by and pick you up at eight?"

"Sure, I'll be ready — but meet me at the end of the block. I don't want to get Mr. Tucker stirred up again." Paula said good-bye and hurried to get ready, eager to see Garth and feeling suddenly refreshed.

But her buoyant mood was dimmed when she stepped outside and saw Mr. Tucker tinkering with his car. He glanced at her briefly, his features puckered in disapproval. Tucker's four-year-old grandson noticed the expression and mimicked it, topping it off by sticking his tongue out at her.

Monkey see, monkey do, Paula thought sourly as she walked away, glad she'd told Garth not to meet her in front of her house.

The car pulled up just as Paula reached the corner. Paula kissed Garth lightly on the cheek as she slid inside.

"Hi, beautiful," he said, smiling.

"Thanks," she said, smiling back.

They drove in silence for a while. Then Paula

started to tell him about some of the things that had happened the day before. He was shocked to hear that someone had deliberately tampered with her car.

"That's amazing," he said, shaking his head in disbelief. "I think it rules out Coralynn, though. It's not that I'd put it past her — I just don't think she knows enough about cars."

"What about Virgilia?" Paula asked after a moment. "Maybe she's the one who's responsible for the other pranks, too."

"Virgilia? Are you kidding? Why would she do those things?"

"I don't know — I've been trying to figure out a reason," Paula admitted.

Garth glanced at her. "I don't get it."

"I know it's hard to imagine — but something really strange happened yesterday." She told him about the scene at Virgilia's locker. "What would she be doing with a bunch of bugs you'd buy in a novelty store?"

"So you think Virgilia bought those fake bugs and a battery-operated rat so she could have fun scaring the pants off people?"

Paula stared at Garth. She could tell that he was fighting to keep from laughing. It didn't take long before he couldn't control himself any longer.

"Would you mind letting me in on the joke?" she asked when he calmed down for a moment. The question started him laughing again and it took another minute before he could answer her.

"I'm not laughing at you, I promise. It's just

that — I've known Virgilia for most of my life. Virgilia's idea of a good time is to attend a lecture — or go to a symphony or something. It just strikes me as funny to picture her thinking up ways to scare people."

Garth turned into the school parking lot.

"Besides," he continued, "I happen to know that Virgilia uses those bugs to illustrate some of her science projects. I've seen them — they're really good."

Okay, Paula thought as she got out of the car. Frankly, I'm glad the evidence doesn't point to Virgilia as the culprit. . . . But now what?

Chapter 22

Now what? That question still plagued Paula as she moved among the tables at the Dog House later. It was slow for a Friday, she noticed. I guess the rat made a lasting impression, she reflected as she stacked additional napkins in the dispensers.

In the past hour and a half they'd had only one customer — a quiet, elderly gentleman who ordered a cup of tea and studied a road map. He's just passing through . . . if he were from around here he might not have come in at all, Paula thought.

She was glad that Cookie was working that day, too. At least they could talk once in a while to relieve the monotony. But Trixie didn't like to catch them talking.

Every once in a while Trixie would poke her head out of the kitchen to see how many customers there were. When she saw that there weren't any more than the last time she looked, she'd remind Paula and Cookie to get to work because they weren't being paid to stand around. Then she told Cookie to stay behind the counter and Paula to take care of the tables.

The evening dragged on. It was near closing time when Paula was surprised to see Mr. Woods walk in.

"Miss McLaughlin, Miss McLaughlin," he called cheerily as he scurried toward her. "I brought something for you! Ah, I see another one of my students. Hello, Angelina!" he called, waving at Cookie. Paula watched in amusement. Cookie hated being called her real name, Angelina.

Mr. Woods took a seat at the counter. "Well, well, Patricia, I've been meaning to visit your establishment," he called to Trixie. "Patricia and I were classmates in high school," he told Cookie and Paula.

Trixie came out of the kitchen scowling. "I remember you. Alo-Wishy-Washy-Woods, we used to call you," she said, breaking into a grin. "Glad to see you, but call me Trixie, Al, not Patricia."

Paula stared, a little shocked at Trixie's way of greeting an old classmate.

"Why of course, Trixie it is — I had forgotten that you had a nickname you liked. Fortunately, mine didn't stick," Mr. Woods added dryly. "Now, do you serve soyburgers, Trixie? I'm in the mood for a soyburger and a lovely green salad with gobs of tofu and tahini dressing." Mr. Woods pressed his hands together in anticipation.

Paula watched as Trixie regarded him coldly. "Listen, Al — I don't serve any soyburgers or any of that other stuff you were talking about. I serve only normal food — doughnuts and pancakes, bacon and eggs, burgers and fries," Trixie said, and walked back into the kitchen.

Mr. Woods turned pale, Paula noticed, apparently at the thought of eating any of those things. "I'll just have a cup of coffee," he told Cookie. "I allow myself that. Paula, you said something about trying out for the Spring Musical. I just happened to be passing by, and I have a script with me. I thought you might like to have it. Be careful with it, though — copies cost money, you know."

Paula accepted the script. "Thanks — what a surprise! I can start looking at it right away!"

"My pleasure," Mr. Woods said gallantly. "Perhaps I've been a bit too hard on you — but make sure you keep paying attention in class!"

Mr. Woods is quite a character — but he's really pretty nice, Paula thought as she bustled around cleaning up. He must have found something he could eat because he has a plate in front of him, she noticed as she glanced his way.

Paula hurried to finish cleaning up, and she didn't think about Mr. Woods again for a while — not until she heard him groan and double over, clutching his stomach.

Trixie ran out of the kitchen and looked at him in horror. "Oh, no!" she cried over and over again, wringing her hands. "Al, don't get sick — please don't get sick. Cookie — don't just stand there, call an ambulance."

Moments later paramedics took Mr. Woods away on a stretcher, still howling in pain.

"Well, we've got to close up early again," Trixie said with a sad note in her voice. She was staring forlornly out the window at the crowd of curious onlookers that had formed at the sight of the ambulance.

"None of the folks out there will be coming inside anyway. Ambulances are always bad for business," she said, shaking her head and stomping back into the kitchen.

Chapter 23

Paula worried about Mr. Woods as she drove home. The paramedics who had taken him to the hospital hadn't been able to tell her what was wrong with him. They said that would require a thorough examination. In her mind's eye Paula kept seeing him lying on the stretcher.

Was Mr. Woods another victim of a strange "accident"?

Had he been poisoned?

If he had been poisoned, would he die? Paula didn't want to think about it, but she couldn't help it.

The car swerved suddenly, and Paula narrowly missed hitting another car. She reminded herself that her mother's car was difficult to steer. It required constant pressure on the wheel, even on the straightaway.

She hit the brakes and pulled up for a red light. As she waited for it to change she decided on a plan.

It's not up to me to play detective, and it's foolish to try. I'm going to the police right now and tell them everything that's happened. They'll know how to handle it. They'll do something.

Unless, of course, they thought she was crazy.

But I'm not crazy.

Sure, said a little voice in the back of her mind. That's what they always think — it's not me, it's the rest of the world. . . . She could imagine a friendly officer in blue telling her to calm down.

I'm going to take my chances and go to the police anyway, she told herself firmly.

The light changed, and Paula stepped on the gas. She watched for the turn-off she'd have to take to the police station. But as she approached it, she hesitated.

Suddenly the idea of going to the police seemed much scarier than it had moments ago when she'd gotten the idea.

She'd have to turn immediately, or keep going. She wavered a moment more, and the car behind her honked. Paula passed by the turn-off and kept going.

I can always call the police tomorrow, after I've thought everything over, she told herself.

Right now I'll go home and take a hot bath. Then I'll take a look at the script for the musical.

The musical — darn it! She realized that in all the confusion she'd forgotten about the musical and left the script behind somewhere in the restaurant.

Well — it was late. She could go back and get it tomorrow.

You're always going to "do it tomorrow" she chided herself. Then you think about it — but you never get around to doing half the things you day-dream about.

Then another thought occured to her. The script might get thrown out — and Mr. Woods would think that she'd been careless with it. Besides, she could go back and get it right now. She had a key to use when she opened up the place.

At the first opportunity Paula made a sharp turn and headed back to the Dog House.

Somehow, she felt that in a way she was doing something for Mr. Woods by going back for the script. Poor Mr. Woods, worrying about the cost of copies. Well, Paula would be careful with hers.

It's a good thing I've got that key, Paula told herself. Because by now there'll be nobody there.

Paula was wrong.

Chapter 24

The lights were out when Paula drove up to the Dog
House, as she had expected they would be. The Dog
House puppy was still, its neon bark silenced for a
while.

Paula grabbed her flashlight keychain. This
should be enough to find the script, she thought.
It's probably lying behind the counter somewhere.

She got her key ready — but when she tried the
door she found that it wasn't locked.

That's weird, she thought, stepping inside.

She hadn't anticipated how strange the place
would look, empty and dark.

So quiet. The only noise came from the refrigerator motors.

Something told her she should leave right now.

Don't be silly, she said to herself. She stepped
behind the counter and switched on her little flashlight. One by one she searched the shelves.

There was a rustling sound in the corner, and
Paula heard squeaks. Are there mice in here? she
wondered uneasily. She shone the flashlight along

the floor, but she didn't see anything. She resumed her shelf search.

Then a light was switched on in the cellar.

"Who's there?" she called, in a quavering voice. Silence.

An alarm was beginning to sound in Paula's mind. *Run!*

But suddenly the lights in the cellar snapped off.

Panic shot through Paula's brain. She jumped and dropped the flashlight from her hand. She heard it fall on the floor with a cracking sound, and its tiny bulb went dark.

Then there was the sound of feet running up the stairs. Paula turned around quickly and fumbled along the wall with outstretched hands. In the darkness she had lost her sense of direction.

She could hear that the runner had reached the top of the stairs now and was coming toward her. Paula tried to run for the door but she kept banging into the counter. Finally she tried to push herself over it.

Then someone grabbed her arms roughly from behind.

They struggled. Whoever was after her was very strong. They kept turning her around and around until she started growing dizzy. Her heart was pounding wildly.

Paula had an odd sensation that she knew the person. She could hear their breathing and hoped that meant that they were growing tired.

Her outstretched hands reached the open space between the counter sections. Paula surged forward, but her hip bone struck hard against something solid. The pain shot through her. For a moment, she was unable to move.

In that moment, she was thrown against a wall, and her hands were tied behind her back. She broke free again, but now that she was unable to stretch out her hands it became almost impossible to avoid running into things or to keep her balance. She was afraid to move too fast for fear of falling over forward or backward.

Her pursuer caught her again easily. This time a blindfold was tied over her eyes.

Paula stood still, feeling completely out of breath. Who was it? she wondered frantically.

Whoever it was paced back and forth again and again, hitting things as they passed by in the dark. Then a light snapped on. Paula could see that much through the blindfold. Cautiously she moved her hand behind her. She felt the outside edge of a sink and realized that she hadn't run toward the door after all. She had run into the kitchen.

Finally, the person spoke.

"Scared?"

Oh, no, Paula thought. It's not possible —

"A kitchen can be a scary place," the voice went on. "There's glass . . ." A glass shattered against the wall with a threatening, splintering sound.

"There's fire . . ." Paula heard the flames from the stove flare up with a loud *whooosh!*

"Things fall . . ." the voice continued, and Paula heard the sound of a heavy iron skillet thudding to the floor so near her feet that she jumped.

". . . and things break!" Stacks upon stacks of plates were pushed to the floor. Paula felt shards of crockery stinging her legs, and she jumped.

"Keep still — don't you move!" her captor bellowed in a rage.

Paula stood frozen, paralyzed by terror. She knew that voice all right. Yes. It was too horrible to be true, yet it was.

It's Trixie!

Chapter 25

Frantically Paula worked her hands against their bonds. What had Trixie used to tie them with? she wondered. It's . . . yes, it's an apron, she realized.

Trixie was talking like a lunatic, faster and faster, each sentence screeching into the next.

"You all think you're better than me, and why? Because you're going to graduate from high school and go on to new experiences, be big shots." Her voice became a sneering, high-pitched singsong. "Dumb old Trixie didn't finish high school. Dumb old Trixie's just a waitress."

"Trixie, *no*," Paula started to protest. "Nobody thinks that — "

"*Shut up!*" Trixie screeched. "I heard you talking that night, you and that Garth, making your big plans for the future — and how glad you were you wouldn't have to be a *waitress* anymore. And then — " *smack smack smack*, Trixie made loud kissing sounds.

"You're all alike, I can tell," Trixie rattled on. "When you first start it's 'Trixie show me this,' and

'Trixie show me that.' You don't know how to do anything and you're *scared*. How about it, kiddo — are you scared now?"

There was a whirring sound as Trixie turned on the electric slicing machine.

Paula felt a chill in her heart. She remembered the spinning circular blade with its glinting edge of steel. The thing was deadly. It could cut through bone.

She tugged desperately at the apron tying her hands. The whirring of the electric slicer was like background music for a bad horror film, she thought. Except this time I'm the star.

Trixie began making her way across the kitchen toward Paula. Pulling and twisting, Paula felt the bond coming loose. As Trixie got closer Paula pulled so hard that it felt as if her wrists would snap — and then her hands were free. Quickly she pulled off the blindfold.

There were only seconds to size up the situation. Paula realized that she'd have to put something between her and Trixie — but what? She scanned the kitchen while her mind raced to evaluate the protective potential of each item.

The pots and pans were already strewn around on the floor, and so were the dishes. She didn't want to start throwing knives — she didn't want to give Trixie any ideas.

Then she saw cartons of eggs, dozens of them, piled high at the end of a steel table. She dashed over and began ripping open the cartons and hurling them on the floor. In a few seconds the floor was covered with a slimy mass of raw eggs and shells.

Trixie saw what was happening, but not fast enough to avoid the mess. She lost her footing and slid halfway across the kitchen. It stopped her all right — but now Trixie and the slimy egg mess were in between Paula and the kitchen doorway.

Paula tried to make a detour, but Trixie was already getting to her feet. The woman staggered toward the doorway, walking stiffly to avoid slipping on the eggs. Soon she was standing beside the butcher chopping block that was just inside the kitchen doorway. Above the chopping block was a meat cleaver. Trixie grabbed it.

Paula saw that the only place to run was down into the cellar. There she'd be trapped — but the sight of Trixie holding the meat cleaver made her realize there was no choice.

Paula turned toward the basement stairs and started down them as fast as she could go. She didn't get very far, though, before her foot caught on a loose tread. In horror she found she was falling — falling — trying frantically to grab onto something, but her hands felt only air.

Chapter 26

Paula tumbled over and over in dizzying flight, landing in a heap, stunned and disoriented. She tried to focus her eyes, but the room kept spinning. She called out desperately, *"Help!"*

I've fallen — and I can't get up, she realized. I'm at the bottom of the basement stairs. Suddenly she felt Trixie's hand on the back of her collar, and she was being half pushed, half dragged across the basement floor.

She was being pulled toward the huge freezer! Paula tried feebly to push herself up, but she was too shaken from the fall. Trixie shoved her roughly and pulled harder, until she was pulling her through the doorway, into the freezer.

"Maybe you'll make a nice blue-plate special," Trixie giggled as she slammed the door. "Just chill out in there for a while."

Now I finally know what happens to the light in the refrigerator when you close the door, Paula thought grimly as she sagged against a shelf. It was not only cold, it was dark.

From the other side of the door Trixie chattered on, now in a cheery, conversational tone. "Y'know — I was only going to play a few pranks on you smarty pants kids. I hid your stupid script. I was going to give it to you tomorrow — tell you I found it in the garbage where you dumped it by mistake. I couldn't wait to see you try and figure that one out!" she giggled merrily. "But you had to come back!"

Paula imagined Trixie doing her switch from grin to scowl. "Well, now that you're here you might as well stay a while. *Ta-ta* and *keep cool!*"

Paula heard Trixie's giggling fade away as her footsteps retreated up the stairs. Soon all she could hear was the steady whirring of the ceiling fan.

It's the darkness that's going to make me crazy, she thought, feeling the tide of panic rising. Her breath came in short little gasps, and she was aware that her heart was pounding. In spite of the chill, sweat was standing out on her brow.

She opened her mouth to scream — when somehow a voice inside her head yelled *stop!*

Paula began grinding her teeth together. Yes — I've got to try to keep calm. It's the only chance I've got to find a way out of this. Otherwise it's a matter of which happens first — run out of oxygen — or freeze to death.

Okay, okay — *think!* There's a light switch, I remember. The light goes off automatically but there is a switch and I can find it . . . and *wait!* There's a safety handle — Trixie showed me that the first day.

She got to her feet unsteadily. It hurt — but apparently nothing was broken. It's a miracle, she thought. Still, I'd rather not know how bad the bruises are.

She felt her way along cautiously. Let's see — the fan is behind me, so the door is on the opposite side, and the light switch is right beside it. After a few fumbling tries she found the switch and clicked on the light.

Success! Now to turn the safety handle and be home free.

But as Paula looked along the door to locate the knob, her heart sank.

Clever, clever Trixie. You thought of everything, she thought sadly, seeing the hole where the handle had been removed.

Now what? she wondered, struggling to control her terror. If only there were something that could force the door open — something I could push into the hole against the lever.

She pulled a pen out of her jacket pocket. The pen was long enough — but it wasn't strong enough. The plastic simply snapped in half.

Paula stamped her foot in frustration.

I've got to do *something*, she thought, pacing around frantically. She began to pile cases of frozen vegetables in front of the fan. At least that would block off some of the cold air.

That's when something about the fan caught her eye. In each corner was a bolt that attached the fan to the main refrigeration unit. Judging from the dimensions of the fan, those bolts must be long.

If I could get one loose it just might do the trick, she thought, stepping cautiously toward the fan. She tried to ignore the nagging little voice that said, "If it doesn't work, what will you do then?"

Two of the bolts were held on so tightly that her fingers just slipped off. But the third — the third began to loosen, and though it was stubborn and rusted, it began to turn. After turning slowly for what seemed like forever with her fingers slipping on the cold metal, she held the long bolt in her hand.

Trembling, she stepped to the door and slid the bolt into the opening where the safety handle should have been.

Praying silently, she pushed the bolt against the lever.

Click.

The door swung open.

Chapter 27

A surge of joy swept over Paula as the huge door opened, making her feel lightheaded. Soon she was stepping through the darkened restaurant.

Careful, she told herself. Trixie might be lurking around somewhere — waiting to pop out with one of her special surprises.

When she reached the parking lot she glanced around nervously. It looks as if Trixie's car is gone, anyway, Paula thought as she reached into her pocket for her keys.

Soon her shaking hands were gripping the steering wheel. Paula was on her way home at last — though she still felt as if she were in a trance.

Any minute now, I'm going to wake up and find out this is only a bad dream — like when I banged my head in gym. If I'd only wake up soon I don't care how bad the headache is — I don't even care if it's a concussion.

This time, though, she knew the nightmare was for real.

She glanced in her rearview mirror to see just

how bad she looked and noticed that the red sedan behind her was tailgating. Just what I need right now, she thought, speeding up slightly.

The red car sped up, too, and the driver began honking furiously.

"Haven't you ever heard of a speed limit?" Paula muttered under her breath. She pressed down on the accelerator a little more. "Is that enough to make you happy?" she said to the reflection in the rearview mirror as she watched the distance widen.

The car behind her flashed its brights on. The glare of the light shone briefly, and then the lights were dimmed again. The driver honked several times.

This guy is some kind of nut, Paula thought with alarm. My nerves are shot as it is. I could have been killed back there in the restaurant, and now this guy is trying to get us both killed on the road.

Paula stuck her hand out of the window and waved the car on ahead. Pass me, please, she prayed. If you're in such an all-fired hurry, pass me.

But the red sedan continued to ride her bumper, honking and occasionally flashing brights. Each time Paula sped up, the other car accelerated until the distance between them was closed once more.

What's he trying to do, drive me off the road?

Is there any way to get away from this maniac?

The traffic was beginning to thicken. Paula started looking for an opening — a chance to move into another lane. Finally she saw a spot and swerved sharply to the left.

Now you can drive some other unlucky soul

crazy, Paula said to herself, looking back at the red sedan in the other lane. She breathed a sigh of relief and began drumming her fingers on the steering wheel.

But soon the car was beside her — and the driver was honking again. Paula turned to look at the driver. He was a pale man with bushy eyebrows — timid-looking rather than fierce. When he saw Paula looking at him he began gesturing wildly.

He looks almost as if he's having a fit, thought Paula.

Maybe he's trying to tell me something.

She kept glancing to her right at the little man who seemed to grow more and more upset. He began jerking his thumb over his shoulder. Paula checked her rearview mirror. There was nothing out of the ordinary.

Paula started to look at the little man again, but the traffic in her lane was speeding up. In a few moments he was swept farther and farther behind her, until soon she lost sight of his car.

Well, I guess that's that, Paula said to herself. She mentally checked over the car. No strange engine noises. No smoke. The brakes seem to be working fine, and I've got plenty of gas. If that funny little man was trying to tell me something is wrong with the car, I sure can't figure out what it is.

When I get home, I'm going to call Garth, no matter how late it is. I only hope I don't wake up his whole family. Then I'm going to call the police. She slowed the car and turned off the main road on to Lonesome Lane.

Paula glanced at her reflection again in the rearview mirror. This time she was able to take stock of the damages. Her hair was in disarray, her blouse was torn, and there was a large smear of black grease down one side of her face. She saw a look in her eyes that she'd never seen before — frightened — watchful. And she saw something else.

The little man *had* been trying to warn her.

Paula fixed her eyes on the road and started humming a little tune. But her teeth were chattering from fear. She didn't want to believe what she had just seen — she was afraid to know if it was truly there. Yet she was more afraid not to know.

Slowly, Paula raised her eyes and gazed into the mirror.

"*Surprise!*" Trixie said.

Chapter 28

It was a miracle that Paula didn't lose control of the car as soon as she caught sight of Trixie's frightening reflection. Trixie's teeth were bared in a wide, red-lipped smile, her red lipstick smeared like a gash across her face. Her red wig was tilted to one side exposing her hair, which stood up like tufts of steel wool. The effect was shocking. Trixie looked like a weird, crazy clown.

Paula had a fleeting impulse to laugh hysterically. It had never occurred to her that the big red beehive was a wig. But there was nothing funny about the glinting edge of the carving knife Trixie held in her hand.

"I heard you start up the basement stairs," Trixie giggled. "I just couldn't believe you got out of there. And here I thought Virgilia was the clever one. So I said to myself, Trixie, I bet that girl will want some company. It's no fun to drive home alone. Then that silly man started honking and almost spoiled my surprise. Well, how about it — are you surprised?"

Paula was afraid her heart would stop beating. Her eyes flickered between the narrow roadway and the terrifying vision of Trixie.

"Answer me when I ask you a question!" Trixie growled menacingly. "I asked you if you were surprised!"

"It's a big surprise, Trixie," Paula whispered. Her chest felt so tight it was difficult to get the words out.

Trixie chuckled appreciatively. "I knew it — you kids think you're so smart — so clever — but old Trixie can outfox you every time."

"That's right, Trixie," Paula said, almost inaudibly. "Trixie — put the knife down — please."

Trixie shook her head. "Uh-uh, not just yet. Too bad, hon, I'm going to have to get rid of you, just like I got rid of that big-mouth Jeff what's-his-name, last year," she giggled.

"I outsmarted 'em all with that one. They never figured out that he stopped by the Dog House before he headed over to the drive-in. 'Course I used a poison that takes a while to work. I didn't want him dropping dead at my place!" This was followed by a loud guffaw.

Then Trixie's tone turned nasty. "I had to teach him a lesson. Every time he came in he was bragging about that big college scholarship he had — and wearing that letter sweater. Always talking like it made him better than other people. One day I got fed up and decided he had to go.

"You weren't nearly so bad as he was," Trixie raved on. "I would have stopped after playing a couple of more pranks on you. But you had to come snooping around — sticking your nose in where it didn't belong." Trixie leaned forward, bringing the knife closer to Paula's neck.

Paula gritted her teeth and floored the gas pedal. The car lurched forward, bouncing roughly over the dirt road. Frantically, Paula jerked the steering wheel right and left, fighting to keep from losing control of the car.

Trixie was thrown from side to side in the backseat. Her expression was one of disbelief. "You're crazy!" she shrieked. "You're trying to get us both killed!"

Oh, and I'm the only one who is supposed to get killed, right? Paula thought. The car bounded into the air as it thudded over a series of bumps. Paula could feel that they were headed for disaster. She swerved sharply to avoid running into the trees, and slammed on the brakes. She hoped that she could get out of the car and make a run for it.

As the car skidded to a halt, Paula could feel the seat belt digging into her. Trixie was pitched forward, almost into the front seat. The knife was thrown from her hand and a strange thought flashed through Paula's mind.

I hope the upholstery isn't cut.

The knife thudded to the floor somewhere. Paula grabbed for the door handle and was about to jump out of the car when the sound of Trixie's crying stopped her.

She turned and saw Trixie slumped in a corner of the backseat. She seemed to have shrunk in size.

The rage had gone out of her, and she held her head in her hands, sobbing like a little girl.

"I'm so tired, I'm so tired," she babbled. "Year after year it's the same thing. A new bunch of kids from the high school. More part-time help to train. Explaining over and over and over again how to do this and how to do that. But they still think they're smarter than dumb old Trixie the waitress."

"But we don't think that at all, Trixie. Everyone looks up to you," Paula began. But Trixie wasn't listening. She was gathering steam again.

"Big deal, so I dropped out of high school. I wanted to have fun. But it isn't any fun. Always a bunch of smart-alecky customers from over at the high school. They graduate and some new ones take their place. Always training a new bunch of klutzy kids. And all the time I'm stuck with the dirty plates and the grease — *work, work, work,* and *cheap tippers!*" Her voice had reached a roar.

But Trixie didn't go off into hysteria again as Paula feared she would. Suddenly it seemed as if all the wind had been knocked out of her, and she hid her head in her hands.

"How could I do all those things? Oh, no, oh, no, they'll find out now and I'll get in trouble," she sobbed.

Oh, boy, will you ever be in trouble all right, Paula thought. You're worried about getting in trouble, Trixie? Well, you've been a very bad girl.

But Paula couldn't help feeling sad as she looked at Trixie sobbing away. Poor Trixie, you wanted to get back at everybody who thought you were dumb for being a waitress — and the only one who thought that was you.

Cautiously, Paula started the car. She was relieved that it would still run.

Trixie continued to sob all the way to the police station. All along the way Paula kept asking herself the same question.

Where did the knife go?

Chapter 29

"Can you pass the popcorn?" Garth asked.

Paula handed the bowl to Cookie, who passed it on. "You know — I can't believe the whole thing happened just last night," Paula said, looking around at her friends. "A few hours ago I never imagined I'd be safe again, sitting in my living room and talking about it like it was a — a movie."

"Well — it sure sounds like a horror movie, all right," Virgilia said solemnly. "What *I* can't believe is that you drove her to the police station. I'd have been scared out of my wits."

"I was." Paula nodded vigorously. "But what could I do? I couldn't sit out there in the middle of Lonesome Lane and wait to see what she'd do next."

"I'll say," Cookie agreed, reaching for a handful of popcorn.

Garth squeezed Paula's hand. "You sure did some cool thinking, getting yourself out of that freezer."

"*Cool* thinking, Garth? I guess you were making a joke?" Cookie smiled mischievously.

"Oooh, that was bad, Cookie," Garth laughed.

"So anyway," Paula broke in, "while we were driving to the police station Trixie seemed really sorry about what she did. She confessed about a lot of the pranks."

"So, let us in on it," Cookie prompted.

"Well — like the weird phone calls, and the messages on my answering machine, for one thing. And the scary messages written on the checks — you know, *Better watch out or you'll have a bad accident*. She didn't mean that one especially for me . . . it was for whoever found it. Trixie thought it would be a customer."

Cookie made a face. "It's so strange . . . we had no idea Trixie felt the way she did . . . that everybody thought they were smarter — or that she was plotting against us. I liked Trixie a lot, and I thought she was crazy about her customers."

"That's just it," Garth interjected, "she *was* crazy."

"It's too bad," Paula said sadly. "Trixie just had things all mixed up. You know, Cookie, I wonder why Trixie never played any pranks on *you*."

Cookie looked thoughtful for a moment. "Maybe it was because she thought I was going to come and work at the Dog House full-time — you know, sort of follow in her footsteps. Trixie got really angry with me when I told her I wasn't going to take that manager job. I tried to explain to her why I wanted to finish high school first and maybe even go on to college — but she wouldn't listen to me. I guess she thought I let her down — like everybody that worked there for a while and left."

Virgilia nodded.

"Don't you want to hear what else Trixie confessed to?" Paula asked.

There was a chorus of yeses.

Paula was enjoying the attention, so she hesitated a moment before saying, "Well, there was *the rat!*"

"*The rat!*" her audience repeated in unison, before bursting into laughter.

"I don't even know why I'm laughing — it was so terrible." Paula paused, trying to catch her breath as she wiped tears from her eyes. Then she looked at Virgilia. "But the sight of you holding that thing by the tail and singing 'Mickey Mouse'!" She doubled over with laughter again.

Virgilia grinned. "I told you the thing didn't look right to me to begin with, when it was on the plate. I'd seen those rats in novelty stores when I'd buy bugs and worms for my science projects." She was quiet for a moment. "I guess it was Trixie who stole my computer discs. She probably just took them out of my book bag while I was working. Anyhow — I've redone all the work."

Paula sighed along with her. "It sure sounds like a lot of work, Virgil," she said sympathetically. "But getting back to the rat for a moment, and this time I mean our rat Coralynn, it looks like she's the one that trashed my gym locker. Trixie swore that she never went sneaking around the school. Too bad I can't prove it."

"Right," Cookie agreed, "it's too bad, but you can't." She shook her head. "Trixie must have really lost it if she couldn't see how she was hurting her own business with all those accidents."

"I wonder what's going to happen to the Dog House — if it will be closed for good or what?" Cookie continued. "I wasn't working there for fun — I really needed the money."

"I heard Trixie had a partner somewhere," Virgilia added.

"Well — I guess we'll find out soon," Paula spoke up. "By the way — I didn't tell you the most important thing yet. Trixie told me that she's the one who poisoned the guy who died in the drive-in. She said all his blabbing about his scholarship really got to her — and she decided he had to go."

"Whew!" Garth shook his head in amazement and looked down at the rug.

Everyone sat in silence for a moment, contemplating this latest piece of news.

I bet they're thinking what I'm thinking, Paula said to herself. If Trixie poisoned somebody last year — she could have done it again, any time. We were in danger every single day that we worked at the Dog House — and so was everyone who walked in there.

Chapter 30

A couple of weeks and it almost seems as if the whole thing never happened, Paula told Cookie as she poured water into the big coffee urn. After being closed for a while Trixie's restaurant reopened when her cousin Shep arrived and assumed responsibility for running the Dog House.

A big, gruff fellow who laughed a lot and rarely shaved, Shep had the place running like a top in no time.

"You know, I thought the place would be called the Deadly Diner, and we'd never get any business, but I think people are coming in out of curiosity," Cookie remarked as she wiped off the counter.

"Right," Paula replied. "I like Shep, too, I'm glad he took over. He seems like a real no-nonsense guy."

"Hey, I forgot to tell you — Mr. Woods is going to be okay. Turns out he wasn't part of Trixie's plan at all. Appendicitis."

"I heard he's still going to be doing the Spring Musical," Virgilia chimed in.

"That's right." Paula smiled. "And I knew that

already — because guess who is going to be one of the dancers?" she asked with a knowing grin.

Cookie clapped her hands.

"All right, Paula! I knew you could do it!" Virgilia nodded.

"Well — I didn't," Paula replied. "But I decided I had to try. I had to stop daydreaming about the things I wanted to do — and *do* something."

Paula looked at Garth, who was sitting at the end of the counter munching on a grilled cheese sandwich. He caught her eye and winked. She winked back.

There's something else that's real, now, and a lot better than a daydream.

But some things never change, she realized, watching Coralynn saunter toward the door, her unpaid check still on the table. Trixie had always let Coralynn freeload, and she was still at it.

Not this time, however.

Shep came barreling out of the kitchen and grabbed the check from the table. "Forget something?" he asked, holding it in front of Coralynn's face.

Paula saw Coralynn jump in surprise. "What?"

"Coralynn, darling 'niece,' I reminded you of that the last two times you were here."

"But, Uncle Shep — I don't see why I have to," Coralynn whined. "Aunt Trixie let me come in for free all the time. Besides," she pouted, "I don't have any money, so what can I do?"

In reply Shep grabbed Coralynn by the arm and pulled her roughly toward the kitchen.

"Come with me, young lady — I've had enough of this foolishness. You'll do what anyone else does if they don't pay the bill. You'll wash dishes." He led Coralynn to the sink and motioned the dishwasher aside.

"Take a break!"

"Well?" Shep stared at Coralynn, who was a picture of disbelief, with folded arms.

"B-but," she sputtered.

Paula smiled and handed her the soap.

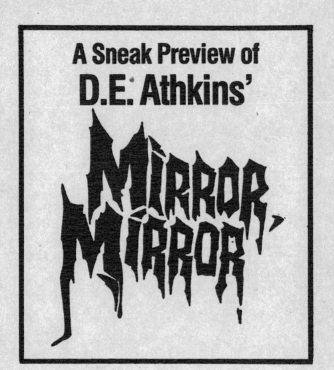

A Sneak Preview of
D.E. Athkins'

MIRROR, MIRROR

MIRROR, MIRROR

A few days later Dore was sitting in the bleachers after school, watching the football team practice. Randy thought she'd come because of him. He was definitely hotdogging it. But it wasn't Randy she was watching; it was Corbin.

It was Corbin she wanted.

Randy was entertaining enough, more acceptable than Tom (she smiled at *that* memory), but she was getting tired of listening to his play-by-play commentary on everything. Even — her lip curled unconsciously — even when they were steaming up the windows of the car. She was ready to move on.

And Corbin, in addition to being definitely smoother than Randy, smoother than ice on glass, was also attached to Mary.

Her glance shifted to the cheerleaders, earnestly practicing their routines on the apron of grass beyond the track that encircled the scrimmage field. Mary had her hands cupped, ordering the other cheerleaders around.

Cheerleaders! The little curl stayed in Dore's lip. She was going to spike one cheerleader's rah-rahs. She was going to make one cheerleader take notice. And be very, very unhappy.

Corbin went over to the sidelines and took off his helmet to get a drink.

Look at me, she willed him. *Look at me.*

Almost as if he heard her thoughts, he raised his head slowly. She looked down at him and shifted her position slightly, stretching her long, long legs out as if she were trying to get more comfortable. Then she smiled.

He stared at her for a moment longer. Finally, slowly, he smiled back. He tossed down the water and turned away.

But she could tell by the way he walked that he knew she was watching.

Far across the field, the cheerleaders began a series of complicated tumbles. All except one. The one who'd been calling the shots only a minute before had stopped, hands on hips, and was standing looking out across the field.

Had Mary been able to see what had just happened?

Dore hoped so.

A short time later, Dore stood waiting by the back steps of the school. It was getting late. Dark. She shivered a little in the cool evening air.

Where was Randy?

The door opened, and another stream of people came out.

Mary Moran and Corbin were among them. This time, he didn't take so long to smile back at her. He was still smiling when Mary came up and took his arm. She stood on tiptoe and kissed his cheek and began to lead him away. Dore saw Corbin look back over his shoulder. At her. She met his eyes without smiling, without blinking.

Then they were gone.

The streetlights came on. The sound of people's voices, getting into cars, leaving, drifted back to her.

Arms closed around her. Pulled her close.

Suffocatingly close.

"Randy?" She tried to turn.

But she was held in a grip of iron. A vise.

Something flashed in front of her eyes. Claws.

She tried to pull her hands free, tried to protect herself.

The claws bore down, down.

To her face.

Chapter 8

Her face was wet. Sticky.

Hands touched her cheek. She swung wildly.

"Hey. Hey!" said a familiar voice.

The giddy blackness swam away from her and she saw . . .

"Stan?"

"Shh," said Stan. "You fell. Did you trip?"

"No. Someone . . ."

"What's going on?" Randy's voice. Now in the half-light she could see him and the shadows of the last of the football players emerging from the building.

"What happened — wow. Look at her sleeve!"

And, then, suddenly, there was Gwen. Gwen was leaning over her. Gwen was helping her sit up. Dore looked up at Gwen. Then down at her arm. The sleeve of her jacket was torn. Shredded.

"You're lucky," said Stan.

"Lucky?" croaked Dore.

"That you landed on your shoulder."

"They should put better lights out here," said Gwen indignantly. "Someone might really get hurt!" Someone did, Dore wanted to say. But she wasn't. Was she?

"Are you okay?" asked Randy, echoing her thoughts.

"I . . . yes . . ." She was so confused.

"I'll take her," said Randy.

"She's fine where she is," said Stan, tightening his arm on her shoulders.

"I want to get up," she said.

It would have been funny if she hadn't felt so weak. So sick. Funny the way they both grabbed onto her, helping her up. Gwen began gathering up her books.

"C'mon," said Randy.

"I . . ."

"Dore." That was Stan.

"Stan? Stan, what are you doing here?"

"I'm the team mascot, remember? We were working out some drills. With the cheerleaders."

"Oh."

"I'll get you home," said Randy. "You just need to rest."

"Wait. Stan . . . Randy." She stopped. Moaned.

"My car is right here," said Randy.

Surprisingly, Gwen intervened. "I'll take Dore home. You guys can work this out later."

This was Gwen talking? Dore's head spun.

"Stan . . . please," she whispered. Stan let go of her arm and stepped back. "I'll call you," he said.

Beside her, Randy gave a little snort of laughter. "I'll *see* you," he said with heavy emphasis.

"C'mon, Dore," said Gwen, grabbing the arm that Stan had released. The unshredded arm.

"Okay," she said obediently.

As she let Gwen lead her to her car, she heard Randy's voice raised behind her. "She fell. What're you all waiting for? Blood?"

Suddenly, Gwen was a tower of strength. It was Gwen who got them past Dore's mother, full of cheerful greetings, happy talk. Gwen who shepherded Dore upstairs. Gwen who got something for Dore to drink and settled her in her bed.

Good old Gwen, thought Dore. She could imagine having to talk to her mother: "Dore, what happened?" "Well, Mother, guess what, something tried to claw me to death while I was waiting for Randy after football practice."

No. To her mother, that would just mean she shouldn't be going out with Randy at all. In fact, her mother didn't *know* she was going out with Randy, exactly.

Although Dore could tell she was suspicious.

No, thought Dore, I don't want Mother worrying.

Like worrying me to death. . . .

The phone began to ring as she lay back gratefully on her bed without even turning on the light.

"I'll get something to drink," Gwen had just said, slipping out.

Still feeling as if she were moving in slow motion, Dore picked up the phone.

"Dore."

"Stan." Dore sighed.

"Did you get home all right?"

"I'm home. I'm fine. Thanks for your help."

"Dore, we've got to talk."

"No, we don't."

"Randy's *not* a nice guy, Dore. Talk to some of the other girls he's gone out with. Or talk to some of his friends . . . even his friends will tell you. . . ."

"Stan, please."

"I don't understand what happened to us. One minute, we're fine. The next minute, you're gone. But that's not the issue, really. Not any more . . ."

Ignoring his words, Dore interrupted. "It was time for a change, Stan. What's so hard to understand about that?"

"Dore . . ."

"Stan, enough. Find yourself a nice girl. . . ."

Stan's voice suddenly hardened. "You should listen to me, Dore."

"You don't have anything to say that I want to hear." She hung up the phone. Hard.

And looked up to see Gwen hovering in the door.

Her face was pale. Blanched white. "W-who was it?"

"Stan the man," said Dore scornfully. "He wants to talk."

"Did he . . . did he say what about?"

"As if I didn't know." She closed her eyes. And, immediately seeing the great, gleaming claws of the beast, opened them again.

Gwen set the glasses of diet Coke by the bed. The ice rattled in the glasses like the chatter of cold teeth.

"Thanks, Gwen . . . Gwen. There's not a circus or anything in town, is there? Like with tigers in it, or anything?"

"No. Why?"

"I don't know." Dore half-closed her eyes and leaned back again. Gwen sat down on the edge of the chair. Silence settled over the room.

Dore sat up again. "Gwen. What were you still doing at the school?"

Jumping up, Gwen began to move restlessly around the room. "Oh. I had work. Had to get stuff out of my locker. I . . . hey, what's this?" Gwen held up the silver mirror.

Had Dore left it out? She didn't remember doing that. "It's a mirror," she said shortly. Was Gwen changing the subject?

Gwen tilted the mirror and studied her face in it. "It's heavy. Funny, too. What . . . odd . . . decorations."

"It's old." Now Gwen was making her jumpy. What if she dropped the mirror? Why didn't she just go away?

As if she were reading her mind, Gwen put down the mirror on the desk with a little clunk. "If you're feeling okay, I'll go on."

"Great . . . I mean, thanks and all, but I'm okay now. I'll just chill for a while."

"Yeah. Well. See ya. You want me to turn out the light?"

"Yes. Thanks."

Dore closed her eyes as Gwen left. She heard her footsteps go down the stairs, heard the front door close. Then she opened her eyes again and stared up into the darkness. *Had* she fallen? And, unconscious, imagined the whole thing?

No. It had been real. Real. It had been waiting for her in the dark. Something had come for her out of the shadows.

The darkness in her room suddenly felt eerie and cold. She got up, carefully but quickly, and turned on the lamp. Her hands were still shaking.

"Reality check," she murmured, and sank into the chair next to the bookcase.

No such thing as a beast. No.

The phone rang. She picked it up quickly.

"What's happening?"

"Luci. Hi."

"I didn't know beauty queens ever fell," said Luci. "I thought you had practice in all that sort of thing."

"Word travels fast," answered Dore. "But I didn't fall."

"What happened?"

Dore hesitated. It was so wild. *A wild beast.*

"Well . . . I don't know."

Luci let it go. "You okay now?"

"Fine. No big deal." Trust Luci to keep her curiosity contained, she thought wryly. Dore's eyes fell on her jacket, wadded on the floor by her closet. "Tore my jacket."

"Tough," said Luci sympathetically. "Well, listen, if you need anything."

"Right," said Dore.

"Later," said Luci, and hung up.

Going over to the closet, Dore picked up the jacket. One arm was shredded. Not ripped, or scraped apart, or anything that might have happened in a fall.

Torn to ribbons.

"Damn," said Dore. It could have been her skin. Her skin hanging in bloody strips. Her skin, peeled back to the bone.

Her face.

Hastily she pushed the jacket to the back of her closet. She'd sneak it out the next day, before her mother or Mrs. Bauer found it.

She never wanted to see it again.

For the first time since she'd come in, she became aware of her reflection in the mirrors. She leaned closer.

The claws hadn't touched her face. She was safe.

Picking up the mirror where Gwen had left it, Dore examined her face more closely.

A hideous scar ran from her temple to her chin. It was as white as the belly of a dead fish, with that same gruesome iridescence. It pulled the skin of her face sideways, making one eye wild and skewed. The mouth on the face in the mirror gaped open. Breath fogged the mirror, hiding the face. . . .

The face of a beast.

of her face sideways, turning one eye with that chewed. The could see the face of the other greed and suddenly forced themselves, and at last

The face of a beast.

Chapter 9

No.

No. Her hand jerked with the shock of it, and now her own face looked back at her. It was just a trick of the light, nothing more.

She smiled. If Luci hadn't given her the mirror, she would have thought it was one of Stan's special effects, like his fake blood.

Stan. Slowly her smile faded. Stan. What was it about Stan? Something . . . something she couldn't quite put together.

Like what was Stan doing at the school at that time? Practicing with the cheerleaders, he'd said. But she would have seen him. And she hadn't. No. No, wait, what were Stan and Gwen doing at the school at that time of night?

And why had Gwen been so shaky about that phone call from Stan?

"*I have something to tell you.*" Wasn't that what Stan said?

Stan. And Gwen. Stan and Gwen.

That was it!

Gwen, with her big, sickening worried act. When all she was really worried about was whether Dore knew about her and Stan. About how she had *stolen* Stan from Dore.

Stan and Gwen. Gwen and Stan.

"Surprise, surprise, surprise," muttered Dore. "Surprise, Gwen. . . ."

point® THRILLERS

R.L. Stine
- ☐ MC44236-8 The Baby-sitter $3.25
- ☐ MC44332-1 The Baby-sitter II $3.25
- ☐ MC45386-6 Beach House $3.25
- ☐ MC43278-8 Beach Party $3.25
- ☐ MC43125-0 Blind Date $3.25
- ☐ MC43279-6 The Boyfriend $3.25
- ☐ MC44333-X The Girlfriend $3.25
- ☐ MC45385-8 Hit and Run $3.25
- ☐ MC43280-X The Snowman $3.25
- ☐ MC43139-0 Twisted $3.25

Caroline B. Cooney
- ☐ MC44316-X The Cheerleader $3.25
- ☐ MC41641-3 The Fire $3.25
- ☐ MC43806-9 The Fog $3.25
- ☐ MC45681-4 Freeze Tag (11/92) $3.25
- ☐ MC45402-1 The Perfume $3.25
- ☐ MC44884-6 Return of the Vampire $2.95
- ☐ MC41640-5 The Snow $3.25

Diane Hoh
- ☐ MC44330-5 The Accident $3.25
- ☐ MC45401-3 The Fever $3.25
- ☐ MC43050-5 Funhouse $3.25
- ☐ MC44904-4 The Invitation $2.95
- ☐ MC45640-7 The Train (9/92) $3.25

Sinclair Smith
- ☐ MC45063-8 The Waitress $2.95

Christopher Pike
- ☐ MC43014-9 Slumber Party $3.25
- ☐ MC44256-2 Weekend $3.25

A. Bates
- ☐ MC45829-9 The Dead Game (12/92) $3.25
- ☐ MC43291-5 Final Exam $3.25
- ☐ MC44582-0 Mother's Helper $2.95
- ☐ MC44238-4 Party Line $3.25

D.E. Atkins
- ☐ MC45246-0 Mirror, Mirror $3.25
- ☐ MC45349-1 The Ripper (10/92) $3.25
- ☐ MC44941-9 Sister Dearest $2.95

Carol Ellis
- ☐ MC44768-8 My Secret Admirer $3.25
- ☐ MC44916-8 The Window $2.95

Richie Tankersley Cusick
- ☐ MC43115-3 April Fools $3.25
- ☐ MC43203-6 The Lifeguard $3.25
- ☐ MC43114-5 Teacher's Pet $3.25
- ☐ MC44235-X Trick or Treat $3.25

Lael Littke
- ☐ MC44237-6 Prom Dress $3.25

Edited by T. Pines
- ☐ MC45256-8 Thirteen $3.50

Available wherever you buy books, or use this order form.